D0338349

The Lemonade War Series: Books 1-4

The Lemonade War
The Lemonade Crime
The Bell Bandit
The Candy Smash

Praise for the Lemonade War Series

The Lemonade War
"Funny, fresh, and plausible." —*School Library Journal*

The Lemonade Crime
★ "Riveting." —*Booklist,* starred review

The Bell Bandit
"Davies portrays Evan and Jessie with subtlety and conviction. . . .
A fresh addition to a well-written series." —*Booklist*

The Candy Smash

by
Jacqueline
Davies

WITHDRAWN
ROWLETT PUBLIC LIBRARY
3900 MAIN STREET
ROWLETT, TX 75088

Houghton Mifflin Books for Children
Houghton Mifflin Harcourt
Boston New York

Copyright © 2013 by Jacqueline Davies
Illustrations by Cara Llewellyn

All rights reserved. For information about permission to reproduce selections from this book, write to Permissions, Houghton Mifflin Harcourt Publishing Company, 215 Park Avenue South, New York, New York 10003.

Houghton Mifflin Books for Children is an imprint of Houghton Mifflin Harcourt Publishing Company.

"Mushrooms" from THE COLOSSUS AND OTHER POEMS by Sylvia Plath, copyright © 1957, 1958, 1959, 1960, 1961, 1962 by Sylvia Plath. Used by permission of Alfred A. Knopf, a division of Random House, Inc. Any third party use of this material, outside of this publication, is prohibited. Interested parties must apply directly to Random House, Inc. for permission.

Additional credits appear on page 232.

www.hmhbooks.com

The text of this book is set in Guardi and Child's Play.
The illustrations are pen and ink.

Library of Congress Cataloging-in-Publication Data
Davies, Jacqueline, 1962–
Candy smash / by Jacqueline Davies.
pages cm — (The lemonade war series ; book 4)
Summary: "Explores the distinctive power of poetry and love—
fourth grade style"— Provided by publisher.
ISBN 978-0-544-02208-9
[1. Poetry—Fiction. 2. Love—Fiction. 3. Schools—Fiction. 4.
Brothers and sisters—Fiction.] I. Title.
PZ7.D29392Can 2013
[Fic]—dc23
2012033305

Manufactured in the United States of America
DOC 10 9 8 7 6 5 4 3
4500406862

For Tracey Adams

an agent with a  the size of a house—

and a Valentine's Day baby, to boot.

Contents

Chapter 1
Zing!

onomatopoeia (n) when a word sounds like the object it names or the sound that object makes; for example: *sizzle, hiccup, gurgle*

If Evan had known what would be hidden in his shoebox later that day, he might not have minded decorating it so much.

But for now, he stared at the box in disgust.

He hated projects like this. Cutting projects, gluing projects. Projects with scissors and paper and markers and tape. Why did he have to *decorate* the shoebox anyway?

"Can I have that?" asked Jessie on her way back to her desk group. She pointed at the ruler on Evan's desk. In her hand, she held her box. All four sides and the top of the box were covered in red construction paper, and the slot on top was outlined with a perfectly measured crinkle-cut rectangle of white paper.

"Why? Aren't you done?" asked Evan.

"No!" said Jessie. "I made spirals for the sides and flowers and hearts for the top." Evan looked over at her desk, which was in the group next to his. Lined up in neat rows were four perfect paper spirals, four curly paper rosettes, and twenty identical paper hearts. Jessie's decorations were so precise, they looked like they came from a factory.

It was at times like this that Evan wished his little sister wasn't in the same fourth-grade class with him. Jessie was good at math and writing and science and just about everything that counted in school. She had even skipped the third grade. Why did she have to be so smart?

Evan slumped a little in his seat. "Go ahead, take it."

Jessie reached for the ruler, then said, "That's sloppy. You should cut the paper so it's even. You want me to do it?"

"No, I don't want your help, Miss Perfect."

Jessie shrugged. "Suit yourself." Then she went back to her seat.

"What are you going to put on your box?" asked Megan, who was returning to her desk on the other side of the room after showing her box to their teacher, Mrs. Overton. Her long ponytail swung from side to side as she walked up to his desk.

Evan felt his face go hot. It was bad enough that his shoebox looked like *nothing*—now Megan Moriarty had to go and notice it.

"I don't know," he said. "I don't like flowers and hearts and things."

"Me neither," said Megan. "I put pictures of cats all over mine. See? This one looks like Langston!"

3

Megan pointed to a picture on her box that looked almost exactly like Mrs. Overton's cat. Langston was a twenty-one-year-old gray Persian who was seriously overweight. There were laminated pictures of him posted all over the classroom, with speech bubbles coming out of his mouth saying COOL CATS READ; NUMERATOR ON TOP, DENOMINATOR ON BOTTOM; and A SIMPLE MACHINE IS A MECHANICAL DEVICE THAT APPLIES A FORCE, SUCH AS A PLANE, A WEDGE, OR A LEVER. In every picture, Langston looked like he'd just coughed up a hairball. Evan's favorite was the one posted right above the daily homework assignment. In giant black letters it said BLEH!

"There are some sports magazines in the Re-use It bin," said Megan. "You want to see if there are any pictures of basketball players?"

"No. Well. I guess," said Evan, embarrassed that he was tongue-tied. When Megan and Evan were in the same desk group, neither one of them could get any work done. Mrs. Overton had called it a lovely problem, and Evan was both disappointed and relieved when she'd changed the seating arrangements.

Whenever he talked to Megan, he got a strange

spinning feeling in his stomach, and it was getting worse every day. It was just like the time two winters ago when he and his mother hit a patch of black ice in their old Subaru. The car spun around three hundred sixty degrees before smashing into a guardrail. No one was hurt, and even the car was okay once it had been repaired, but Evan would never forget that feeling of spinning and spinning completely out of control, waiting for the smash. Being around Megan felt like that.

Evan walked over to the Re-use It bin. It turned out that there were tons of photos of basketball players, including one of Evan's favorite, Rajon Rondo, who was famous for having played the fourth quarter of a playoff game *one-handed* after he dislocated his elbow in the third. Evan quickly cut out five photos and stuck them on the four sides and top of his box.

"Done," he said, putting the cap back on his glue stick and shoving his markers into his desk.

Mrs. Overton, who'd been working at her desk, glanced up at the clock on the wall. "Hey, look at the time." She picked up the *shekere* that sat on the edge of her desk and shook it a few times, making the gentle *sh-sh-sh* sound that meant it was time to transition to a different activity. "We're running late. Leave your boxes on your desks and come to the rug. It's time for the Poem of the Day."

Evan smiled. He would never admit it, but this had become his second favorite part of the day—after recess. Ever since coming back from winter break, Mrs. Overton had taken the time each day to read a poem—just one poem. A serious poem. Not like the silly poems his third grade teacher had read to them last year. Evan liked those, too—they made him laugh—but these poems that Mrs. Overton read were different. They were like music, and they made something deep inside of him go *zing*.

Jessie raised her hand. "Mrs. Overton, can I skip the Poem of the Day so I can work on my newspaper?" Jessie had started her own classroom newspaper called *The 4-O Forum*. She'd already published two issues, and now she was working on the third. She planned to hand out the next edition on Monday, exactly one week from today, which happened to be Valentine's Day. It was a tight deadline, and Evan could tell she was feeling the pressure.

"No, Jess. I'll give you some time during morning recess. For now, come and join the class." When everyone had gathered on the rug sitting cross-legged, Mrs. Overton said, "Today I'm going to read a poem by E. E. Cummings." At the top of a blank page on the classroom easel, she wrote: "E. E. Cummings."

"Is he dead?" asked David Kirkorian. This had become the first question the kids in 4-O asked whenever Mrs. Overton introduced a new poet. Some poets were still alive—like the one who wrote the poem about the tree frog whose throat was swollen with spring love or that other one who wrote about playing basketball with his friend Spanky—but a lot of them were dead. Some of them had been dead for centuries.

"He died about fifty years ago," said Mrs. Overton. A few kids nodded. A long-time dead. The *really* famous poets like William Shakespeare and Emily Dickinson were all dead.

"What's the poem called?" asked Salley.

"It doesn't have a title."

"What do you mean?" asked Jessie. Evan could

see a frown creeping across her face. Jessie did not like poetry, even though she'd won a poetry-writing contest in first grade. It was the only subject in school that Evan had ever heard her say she hated.

"Some poems don't have titles, and E. E. Cummings didn't title most of his poems."

"A poem is no good without a title," said Jessie. She stuck her foot out and retied her sneaker with several sharp, jerky movements. "And what kind of a name is E.E.?"

"It's initials, right?" said Jack. "Like J. K. Rowling. It stands for something."

"Easter Eggs!" said Megan.

"Eleven Elephants!" said Ben.

"Extra Elbows!" said Ryan. He was sitting next to Evan, and he poked his elbow into Evan's chest, which got everyone in the class laughing.

Mrs. Overton admitted that she had no idea what E.E. stood for, but she would find out and report back later. "In the meantime, let's take a look at the poem."

She turned the page on the easel to show the poem that she had copied out earlier.

because it's

Spring
thingS

dare to do people

(& not
the other way

round)because it

's A
pril

Lives lead their own

persons(in
stead

of everybodyelse's)but

what's wholly
marvellous my

Darling

is that you &
i are more than you

& i(be

ca
us

e It's we)

Evan stared at the poem. He hardly breathed. He had never seen anything like it. It was kooky! The way the words fell down the page like rocks tumbling over the edge of a cliff. He liked that "Spring" almost rhymed with "thingS" and the crazy way the tall, proud capital *S*s stood like towers on either side of those words. And why was the word "because" broken up into four pieces? It made him feel as if words weren't so strict and stern and unchangeable as they had always seemed. You could mix them up. You could rearrange them any way you liked. You could play with them—like Legos! You could make them do whatever you wanted. Evan looked at that poem and felt something inside of him go *zing*.

Jessie pointed at the easel. "That is the worst poem I have ever seen in my whole life!" she shouted. "That poem is *all wrong*."

"Wow," said Mrs. Overton. "It sounds like you're having a strong response to this poem, Jessie. Tell us what you think."

"It's full of mistakes," said Jessie, standing up and marching over to the easel. "That *S* is not supposed to be capitalized. You never capitalize just the last letter of a word. And there's a space missing after the parenthesis. And the words 'it's' and 'April' are broken up with no hyphens. And there's no such word as 'everybodyelse.' He just made that up!" Jessie's hands were flying all over the easel, pointing, accusing the poem. She stabbed her finger right into the heart of the poem. "And the word 'I' is always capitalized. *Always.*"

Evan nodded his head. That was the rule.

"So why do you think he did it?" asked Mrs. Overton.

"Because he's dumb," said Jessie, returning to her spot on the rug and plopping down in disgust.

"Well," said Mrs. Overton, "Mr. Cummings graduated from Harvard and wrote his first book when he was twenty-eight. So I don't think he was dumb. Maybe he had a reason for writing his poems in this way. What do you think?"

The kids in 4-O stared at the poem. Some of them moved their mouths silently as they read it to themselves.

"Maybe he was telling a joke," said Tessa.

"Or maybe he was trying to make it look like a kid wrote it!" said Adam. "Maybe he was using a strong *voice,* like you told us about when we wrote our memory stories."

"I bet he just scribbled it out fast like that, and then he didn't bother to check it over," said Paul. Evan knew that Paul hated to copy his first drafts.

"These are all good ideas," said Mrs. Overton. "Anybody else have an idea?"

Evan looked at the poem and thought about the joy he felt when he read it, the looseness and freedom of those crazy mixed-up words, the tumbling recklessness of the way the poem spilled down the page.

"Maybe," said Evan, "he's sort of . . . telling us that there aren't any rules or . . . you know, you don't have to do things a certain way, just because that's how everyone else does them? You know?"

Mrs. Overton nodded her head. "I think that's exactly what Mr. Cummings is challenging us to think about. Rules and conventions. Because what is this poem *really* about?"

The whole class stared at the poem. The room was silent, except for the gentle scrabbling sound of the gerbils in their cage as they chewed on their toilet paper tubes. Slowly, Megan raised her hand, and Mrs. Overton nodded at her.

"It's about love," said Megan.

"That's right," said Mrs. Overton. She turned the heavy paper of the easel so that a fresh, blank page was showing, and then in all capital letters, she wrote,

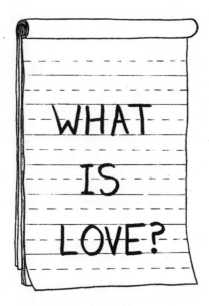

Chapter 2
Smash

smash (n) something that is wildly popular, an unqualified success, a blockbuster

Jessie was the first to come in from morning recess, because Mrs. Overton had said she could return to the classroom five minutes early to work on her newspaper. If it were up to Jessie, she would skip recess every day. It was just a waste of time. She'd rather spend the time reading a book or working on a project. Running around outside! Ridiculous!

And speaking of ridiculous, Mrs. Overton had given them a new assignment: each one of them had to write a poem about something or someone they loved. A love poem! Fourth grade was definitely taking a turn for the worse.

Jessie sat down at her desk and pulled out her reporter's notebook. It was the same kind of notebook her father used: long and thin, spiral-bound, hard-covered, with light blue lines running across each narrow page. She liked using the same notebook he did—liked to think of both of them scribbling notes, writing articles, and changing the world. It made her feel closer to him, even though she hadn't seen him in over a year and he was halfway around the world.

Jessie moved her Valentine's shoebox to the corner of her desk, then tore out four pages from her reporter's notebook and spread them out. She picked up her pencil and wrote a list of the articles that would appear on each page.

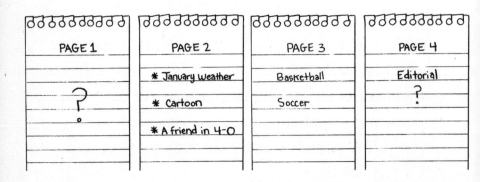

PAGE 1	PAGE 2	PAGE 3	PAGE 4
?	* January weather	Basketball	Editorial
	* Cartoon	Soccer	?
	* A friend in 4-O		

Pages two and three were easy to fill because they contained the newspaper's regular features: the re-cap of the month's weather using all the data that 4-O collected from the weather station mounted on the roof of the gym; a comic strip about an alien, written and illustrated by Christopher Bay; a few sports articles written by different kids in the class who were on various town teams; and Megan's lat-est installment of her advice column, "A Friend in 4-O," the most popular feature in the newspaper.

Dear Friend in 4-O,

Someone in my desk group keeps kicking my chair. I've asked him to stop about a million times, but he still does it. What is his problem????

Signed,
Tired of Being Kicked

Dear Friend in 4-O,

My mom packs snacks I hate. No one will trade with me, these snacks are so bad. I'm always hungry until lunch.

Signed,
Starving and Sad

Dear Friend in 4-O,

I don't get fractions! Seriously! No matter how many times Mrs. Overton explains them, I just don't get them. Help me!!!!

Signed,

The #1 Enemy of Fractions

But Jessie still had no idea what her front-page story would be. And her dad had taught her that the front-page story was the most important part of the whole newspaper. She needed something that would really grab her readers' attention. Something shocking. Something huge. She was determined to make this edition of *The 4-O Forum* a smash, and to do that she needed a prizewinning front-page story.

Jessie knew she had to do some investigative reporting, which is when a reporter uncovers facts that no one else knows and publishes them so the world will be a better place. Jessie's dad had been an investigative reporter before he went back to being a war correspondent. Right now, he was in Afghanistan, but when Jessie was a baby, he had written articles about a big chemical company that was causing pollution and a state senator who was taking bribes. He'd won an important prize for writing the story about the senator, but he'd made a lot of people angry, too. Sometimes Jessie thought *that* was why he left.

Couldn't I investigate something? she wondered. *Uncover a secret, just like Dad?* Too bad her friend Maxwell wasn't here. He was the best spy she'd ever met, not to mention an accomplished thief. If Maxwell were here, they would definitely find something to uncover.

I need a secret, thought Jessie. *And a good one!* She didn't want her front-page story to be a flop—like the last time.

In the last issue of *The 4-O Forum,* Jessie had interviewed the school principal, Mrs. Fletcher. Scott Spencer had said it was the most boring article he had ever *not read.* He pretended to fall asleep with the paper open in front of him. Most of the boys had thrown the paper in the recycling bin without even looking at it, and some of the girls had used theirs to make origami bracelets. The only article anyone had even talked about was the advice column. It made Jessie angry to think about that.

What could she investigate this time? Lots of ideas flashed in her brain: What was in Mrs. Overton's desk drawers? Were the cafeteria hot dogs really made of rubber? Why did the gym teacher leave in the middle of the school year? Who was responsible for the two fire alarms in January? And what made that funny smell down by the school boiler room? The principal said it was an outdated HVAC system that did a poor job of ventilating the school when it rained, but the boys claimed that the custodian had a dead body in there. David Kirkorian was the one who pointed out that the smell had started shortly after the gym teacher disappeared.

But Jessie couldn't actually investigate any of those mysteries. She couldn't break into Mrs. Overton's desk or ask questions about the gym teacher. (She had tried and was told firmly by the principal that it was none of her business.) She couldn't sneak into the boiler room. Jessie shuddered, thinking what it would be like to find a dead body.

Then Jessie thought of something her grandmother had said a few weeks ago when they had seen a news report about protesters occupying the State House: "You can't make an omelet without breaking some eggs."

"What the heck does that mean?" Jessie had asked.

"It means if you want to achieve something important, you might have to make a mess along the way. Ruffle a few feathers. Kick up some dust." Jessie looked blankly at her grandmother. "In other words, Jess, you can't always make everyone happy. Sometimes you have to do what you have to do."

"Grandma," Jessie said sternly. "Are you talking about breaking rules?" The thought of breaking rules made her feel lightheaded.

"Oh, rules," said Grandma. "When you get to be my age . . ."

Jessie stared at the empty pages in front of her and thought of her grandmother's words. Her dad broke rules all the time. He was always sneaking under fences and snooping through trash to uncover a story. Because he wanted to make the world a better place. Because he was a hero.

Just then Scott Spencer burst through the door, followed noisily by half a dozen other kids. Jessie jumped as if she'd been caught red-handed doing something illegal, accidentally knocking her Valentine's shoebox off the desk. It made a strange rattling sound as it fell, and when the lid came off, something unexpected spilled out.

Chapter 3
Mushrooms Take Over the World

personification (n) giving lifelike characteristics to an inanimate object or an abstract
idea; describing an object as if it were alive

Candy!

A box of candy hearts fell out of Jessie's Valentine's Day shoebox, and now all the kids were tearing open the lids of their own boxes and finding
candy, too.

"Sweet!" Evan shouted, scooping up the minia-
ture box of candy conversation hearts.

"Thanks, Mrs. Overton!" said Nina Lee when

Mrs. Overton hurried into the classroom from the hallway. She'd been at the photocopier, making copies of the Poem of the Day.

"Thanks for what?" asked Mrs. Overton.

"The candy!" shouted Jack, holding his box high and rattling it as if it were a maraca.

"Where did this candy come from?" asked Mrs. Overton, looking surprised.

"Who cares?" said Scott, popping three candy hearts into his mouth and crunching loudly.

"I care!" said Mrs. Overton, her voice rising with alarm.

"Hey, look what my hearts say," said Tessa. She held one up. "GREAT VOICE."

"That's so weird!" said Cindy. Tessa had the best singing voice in the whole school. Every year, she sang in the talent show, and it was like watching an episode of *American Idol*.

"Look at this!" said Christopher. He held up his candy heart. "Mine says MASTERPIECE." Christopher was always drawing, and when he grew up he planned to be an artist.

"What does yours say?" asked Jessie, turning to Salley Knight.

"It says BEST LUNCH." No one could argue with that. Salley's mom owned a restaurant, and she always packed the best food in Salley's lunchbox.

"Who brought these candies to school?" asked Mrs. Overton. No one had a clue. "Well, don't eat them," she said, but almost everyone had already popped the sugary hearts into their mouths.

"Should we spit them out?" asked David, sticking out his tongue with the melting candy on the tip of it.

"No! No spitting!" said Mrs. O. "Just . . ." She went to the class phone and made a quick call, then returned to the front of the class. "Let's refocus and get started on our morning work," she said. "We've got a lot to do today."

But it was a good five minutes before everyone stopped comparing the messages written on their candy hearts: BEAUTIFUL HAIR, YOU MAKE ME LAUGH, MATH GENIUS. All of them seemed to say something *about* the person.

All of them except for Evan's. His just said FOR YOU. Well, he didn't care what the candy *said* as long as it was candy. He popped three hearts in his mouth and shoved the box in his back pocket.

On the playground at lunch recess, most of the kids agreed that it must have been Mrs. Overton who had left the candy hearts for them. She had pulled a few sneaky-surprise tricks on them during the year. In January when they were studying the Revolutionary War, she'd had Officer Ken come to school and arrest them all on charges of sedition. During their famous inventors unit, which happened to fall around Halloween, she had left strange things around the classroom (burned-out light bulbs, bits of wire and springs, an antique crank phonograph, and a few ghoulish notes on the blackboard) that seemed to suggest that the ghost of Thomas Edison was haunting 4-O. Evan figured this was just one more prank.

"I'm home!" Evan shouted the next day as he walked through the front door after practice, dropping his basketball in the hall and taking off his sneakers.

"Garage, please," said his mom, pointing to the ball and the shoes. "How was practice?" she asked after Evan came back into the kitchen to grab a snack.

"Great. My team won both scrimmages. Can I eat this in my room?" He held up a banana.

"Yes, but don't leave the peel in your trash can. It'll smell." Mrs. Treski was standing at the kitchen counter, chopping vegetables. She had already made a neat pile of diced carrots and another one of onions, and now she was slicing up celery. That meant enchiladas for dinner! This day just kept getting better and better.

"And don't eat more than that," said Mrs. Treski as Evan headed up the stairs. "Dinner's in an hour."

Evan went up to his room and stuck the Locked sign on the outside of his door before closing it. There weren't any actual locks on the bedroom doors in their house, but Mrs. Treski believed everyone—even kids—had a right to privacy. So they each had a laminated cardboard sign that they could hang on their doors. When the sign was up, it meant everyone else in the family had to act as if the door was actually locked.

Before this school year, Evan had almost never "locked" his door. But now that he and Jessie were in the same class at school—together all day, including lunch and recess—he needed more privacy. On top of that, Grandma had moved in after New Year's, so now the house felt extra crowded. It was starting to become a habit for him to put up the Locked sign.

Evan unzipped the small pocket on the front of his backpack and pulled out a folded piece of paper. Lying on his bed, he began to read the words quietly to himself.

MUSHROOMS
by Sylvia Plath

Overnight, very
Whitely, discreetly,
Very quietly

Our toes, our noses
Take hold on the loam,
Acquire the air.

Nobody sees us,
Stops us, betrays us;
The small grains make room.

Soft fists insist on
Heaving the needles,
The leafy bedding,

Even the paving.
Our hammers, our rams,
Earless and eyeless,

Perfectly voiceless,
Widen the crannies,
Shoulder through holes. We

Diet on water,
On crumbs of shadow,
Bland-mannered, asking

Little or nothing.
So many of us!
So many of us!

We are shelves, we are
Tables, we are meek,
We are edible,

Nudgers and shovers
In spite of ourselves.
Our kind multiplies:

We shall by morning
Inherit the earth.
Our foot's in the door.

It was the Poem of the Day that Mrs. Overton had read to them that morning in class. She always made extra copies and left them on the windowsill so that anyone who wanted to could take one home. On his way out to recess, Evan had told his friends he'd forgotten his gloves. When he went back into the classroom, he'd sneaked a copy of the poem and slipped it in his backpack.

If the whole class hadn't gone over the poem that morning, he would have had trouble reading the words "acquire" and "edible." He wouldn't have known that "loam" was just another word for dirt, or that "discreetly" meant carefully and quietly, while "crannies" were little openings, and "bland" meant boring and tasteless.

But they had gone over the poem, several times, and now Evan could read it confidently to himself, and he loved the way it sounded. He loved to say, "Our toes, our noses / Take hold on the loam." All those "oh" sounds, like marbles rolling across a wooden floor. He liked the phrase "soft fists"—the way one word said the opposite of the other but with almost exactly the same letters! And then when it got to the shouting part, "So many of us! / So many of us!"—Mrs. Overton had had them stand up and raise their arms over their heads to shout out the words—Evan couldn't help but feel the thrill of the mushrooms taking over the world. It was like *Planet of the Apes*—but better sounding. Like music.

Knock. Knock.

Evan kept his eyes on the poem. "Go away!"

"Why?" asked Jessie through the closed door. "Why can't I come in?"

"Because I'm busy."

"Doing what?"

"Jeez, Jessie! If I wanted to have a conversation, I'd leave my door open. Locked means locked!"

"Yeah, but I need help."

"I'll help you later, okay?"

"Oh, fine! You stink," she said. Evan could hear her walking away.

Evan got up from the bed and walked over to his desk. It was piled high with Lego contraptions and loose change and dirty socks and a scuffed-up base-ball and old *Mad* magazines and K'NEX. Evan never worked at his desk. Whenever he had homework to do, he did it at the kitchen table with his mom in the room. That way, she could help him when he couldn't figure something out or give him a pep talk when he felt like tearing his paper to pieces.

Quickly he moved everything onto the floor so that the desk became a wide open space, like a smooth stretch of beach. He sat down and spread his hands across the top. Then he reached down into his backpack and pulled out the stack of Post-it notes that Mrs. Overton had given each of them today during Literacy Block.

Jessie, of course, loved Post-it notes. They were her favorite office product. She had them in every color and used them all over her room to remind her of important things. But Evan had never thought much about them until today when Mrs. Overton had shown the class what they could do.

He looked at the mushroom poem again. He read the first stanza. Just six words. That was all. Anyone could write six words.

Evan stared at the wall and thought about his grandmother.

Well, first of all, she was old. So old that her knees made creaking noises when she stood up. But she still did yoga every day. She said it was good for her balance. She could even stand on one leg like a tree. Sometimes, though, Grandma's brain wasn't balanced. She could forget things. Like Evan's name. He hated when that happened.

Evan peeled off the first Post-it note and stuck it to his desk. He wrote "Grandma" on it. Then he peeled off another one and wrote "tree." Then he wrote four more words, each on its own note.

He lined up the Post-it notes on his desk like soldiers marching in a parade.

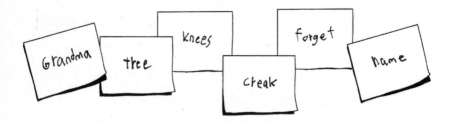

That's not a poem, he thought. *At least, not a good one.* But he liked the way "tree" and "knees" and "creak" sounded together, so he put those words on a line all by themselves.

Then he thought about a tree, and he wrote "tall" and "proud" and "good," each word on its own Post-it note. Just as they'd done in class. The Post-it notes were like blocks, and Evan was good at moving them around, adding new words, new blocks, throwing out the ones he didn't like.

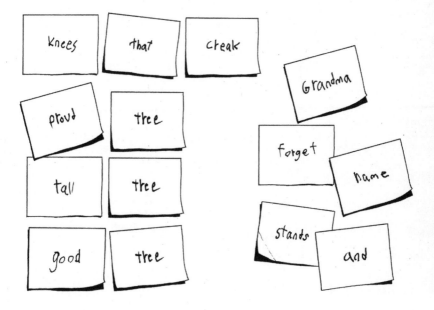

He listened to the sound of the words, whispering them out loud as he moved the Post-it notes all over his desk. He felt like he was building something, watching it grow under his hands.

After half an hour, he stared at the Post-it notes on his desk, then decided to add some parentheses, just like E. E. Cummings.

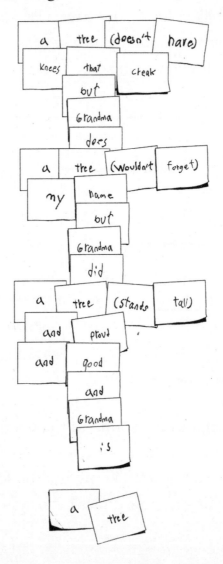

Evan read the words out loud and thought, *That's a poem.*

But was it a love poem? That was the assignment that was due on Friday. Love poems for pets or people or frogs or sunshine or anything else in the world that could be loved. Mrs. Overton had read a love poem to them by Langston Hughes, the poet she had named her cat after. It was a poem about rain, and the last line was "And I love the rain."

Evan wasn't so sure if his poem about his grand-mother counted. Didn't a love poem have to say the word "love" somewhere in it?

Then he thought about E. E. Cummings and how all his poems shouted out, *There are no rules!* and Evan decided that he liked his poem just the way it was, and if you couldn't tell that he loved his grandma, there was something wrong with you.

Suddenly he heard voices in the hallway—Jessie's and someone else's—and then laughter. Evan froze. He knew that laugh. He was in love with that laugh.

Chapter 4
Primary Source

primary source (n) a person with firsthand knowledge of an event; a document written by such a person at the time the event took place

Jessie paused in the school hallway, twisting the strap on her backpack back and forth. She knew the rule. Kids were not allowed in the classroom after school when the teacher wasn't there.

The door was open. She poked her head into 4-O. No one was there. The chairs were all up on the desks. The shades were pulled down for the day. Even the gerbils were in silent hiding, nestled deep beneath the wooden shavings in their cage.

Jessie tiptoed in. Her heart was beating wildly in her chest, and her breathing felt short and choppy. Her heavy backpack pulled on her arms as if trying to hold her back.

She approached Mrs. Overton's desk, which was near the window. On top, there were several neat piles of papers, her pen-and-pencil cup, a shallow dish full of paper clips, two photographs of Langston, and a wilted African violet. Jessie reached out and quickly rubbed one of the plant's leaves between her thumb and fingers, enjoying the velvety feel of the little hairs that covered the leaf. The soft touch of the plant calmed her down. But she didn't have much time. Megan was coming over to her house in half an hour to make their class valentines. And anyone could walk into the classroom at any moment. She would have to be fast. A real pro.

Jessie's eyes scanned the desktop, looking for clues, but what was she looking for? Nothing seemed unusual. Nothing that would reveal Mrs. Overton as the secret person who was leaving candy hearts.

She walked around the desk and took a quick peek in the trash can, spotting only an empty paper cup and an orange peel.

Out in the hall, a locker banged shut with a sharp metallic *clang!* Jessie could hear the sound of a squeaky cart rolling down the hall. She stopped. What if Mrs. Overton came back? Her coat was still hanging on the hook; her purse was underneath the desk. What if the custodian came in to sweep the floor? Would Jessie be expelled from fourth grade?

But she had to be brave. Her newspaper was due in less than a week, and she didn't have a front-page story. There was a secret in 4-O, and it was her job to uncover the truth.

She looked at Mrs. Overton's desk. There was one long, thin drawer in the center and three deep drawers on each side. Jessie wondered whether the drawers were locked. She wondered which drawer was most likely to hold a secret.

Her heart started to beat faster. Her dad did this kind of thing all the time, right? When he told his stories—of classified documents and uncovered clues and secret meetings with sources—he never mentioned being nervous.

She reached her hand toward the top desk drawer.

"What are you doing?"

Jessie's hand jumped back as if bitten by a snake and disappeared behind her back. David Kirkorian stood in the doorway, buried inside his winter coat, woolen hat, and bulky gloves.

"Nothing!" said Jessie. "I forgot my social studies notebook!" This was the excuse she had planned ahead of time, and she had in fact "accidentally" left her notebook in her desk.

"So why are you looking in Mrs. Overton's desk?" David walked up to her and pulled off his hat. "She doesn't keep our notebooks in her desk."

"Why are you even here?" asked Jessie. Was David going to report her to the principal?

"I saw you walk back into the school, and I thought maybe you needed help with something." He took off his gloves and stuck them under his arm. It was warm in the classroom, and his face was beginning to turn bright red with the heat.

"I don't need help," said Jessie. And she didn't. At least not from David Kirkorian, of all people!

He looked at her, then at the wall, then back at her. "I won't tell, Jessie," he whispered. "I'll keep your secret."

"There is no secret!" shouted Jessie. She hurried past him, grabbed her social studies notebook from her desk, and ran out of the room.

When Megan came over to her house, Jessie still felt jumpy. And she still didn't know what her front-page story would be.

"Do you think I can just say that it's Mrs. Overton who's giving out the candy, since it obviously is?" asked Jessie. She and Megan were in the basement, making their cards. Valentine's Day was just five days away, and Jessie was worried about getting all twenty-six valentines done in time. Another deadline! There was so much pressure in fourth grade!

"Isn't that against the law?" asked Megan. "I mean, if it turns out not to be true?" Megan had the messy idea of filling her envelopes with confetti, so she was busy cutting up tissue paper.

"Yeah," said Jessie glumly. It was called *libel,* and you could go to jail for it. "But who else could it be?" Jessie was decorating the edges of her heart-shaped valentines with little glue-on jewels, following a strict pattern—red, silver, purple, silver.

"You never know!" said Megan, and she tossed a handful of confetti into the air so that it rained down on the table.

Jessie brushed the confetti off her side, glad that it hadn't landed in any glue. "Well, if I can't write about the candy hearts, what am I supposed to write about on the front page of my newspaper?"

"You should write about how we're not allowed to include *any* candy in our class valentines this year," Megan said. It was a new rule, and all the kids were against it. She reached for a sheet of pink construction paper and started to cut out a heart. "It's un-American!" Megan's uncle owned a candy factory, so Jessie could understand why she'd be upset.

"That's not a very interesting story," said Jessie. Sure, everyone in 4-O was mad about the new rule, but there was nothing to *investigate.* Candy was bad for your teeth, and grownups cared more about healthy teeth than they did about a kid's happiness. End of story.

"Then we should *make* a story!" said Megan. "We should have a protest. Sign a petition. No! A sit-down strike! We should all refuse to do our homework until that rule is changed!"

Not do homework? Jessie stared at Megan. That sounded completely crazy to her.

"Bad idea," she said. "I need to uncover a *secret.*"

Megan stopped cutting her paper and looked at Jessie. "That doesn't sound very nice. If someone has a secret, they probably don't want you printing it all over the front page of a newspaper."

"Secrets are bad," Jessie said, thinking of the big chemical company and the lying senator. Clearly Megan didn't understand what investigative reporting was all about.

"Some secrets are nice," said Megan, smiling.

There was a clomping sound overhead, and then the door to the basement squeaked open. "Hey, Jess, it's almost dinner," said Evan, but instead of closing the door and going back upstairs, he continued down the steps and wandered over to the table where they were working. "My mom says you can stay, if you want to," said Evan, not even looking at Megan. "What's that?" he asked, pointing to the pile of shredded tissue paper.

Megan grabbed two fistfuls of the confetti and held them up to her head. "It's my new hairdo! Do you like it?"

Evan burst out laughing. Then he grabbed a fistful and held the confetti paper up to his chin. "Do you like my beard?" he asked in a deep voice, and Megan practically fell off her chair, she laughed so hard. Jessie really didn't get what was so funny.

"You guys are weird," she said, bending over her valentine and pressing the last jewel into place. But she wasn't listening to them anymore. She was thinking about the secret in Mrs. Overton's desk drawer.

The next morning an even bigger secret appeared. It popped up in—of all places—the girls' bathroom.

To Jessie, the girls' bathroom was a scary place. Things happened in the bathroom, things that teachers never knew about. Words were whispered, graffiti written, rules broken, trash dumped, water left running, hands left unwashed, noses picked, bodies shoved, names called—anything could happen in the bathroom, because there were no teachers watching. Ever. Jessie had never once seen a teacher enter the girls' bathroom.

For the most part, Jessie avoided the bathroom. She took care of her business at home and, when necessary, in the private bathroom in the nurse's office. But this year, Mrs. Graham had started to "encourage" her to use the girls' bathroom in the hall. At first, Jessie had politely declined, but after a few weeks, it stopped being an offer, and Jessie had to "adapt and evolve," as her mother would say, to this new way of doing things.

Jessie pushed open the old, scarred wooden door of the bathroom and stuck her head in. She didn't mind the bathroom when it was empty, and she didn't mind it when it was jam-packed. But if there were just a few girls in there—especially any of the mean girls from her class last year or the scary big fifth-graders who looked like they were practically teenagers—she would duck back out and look at the artwork in the hallway until the bathroom emptied out.

This morning, the bathroom *was* empty. Jessie hurried to the only stall she ever used, the second-to-last one in the row, and quickly sat down to pee. She liked this stall because the lock worked and because most kids never used it. She had observed this: kids either liked the first two stalls closest to the door or the large, handicapped stall that was like having a room all to yourself. But no one ever chose the second-to-last stall, and that's why Jessie decided it was the safest one of all.

Today, when she sat down, she noticed something new, right in front of her face, written on the door in black ink.

The first thing she thought was that Megan's initials were M.M., but she could tell that Megan hadn't written the letters because Megan always drew curlicues at the ends of her *M*s, and these *M*s were straight up and down.

The second thing she thought was that *E* and *T* were Evan's initials.

Of course, it was a big school with a lot of kids, and all the grades used this bathroom. Maybe *M.M.* and *E.T.* were fifth-graders. That made more sense. Older kids did bad things, like writing on bathroom doors.

When Jessie finished, she left the stall to wash her hands. And then she forgot all about the initials because back in the classroom they were creating models of working lungs using soda bottles and balloons, and Jessie loved making stuff like that.

But later in the morning, when Megan twisted around in her seat to talk to Tessa while Mrs. Overton was giving a math lesson on decimals, Mrs. Overton said, "Megan Moriarity, eyes up front, please!" And Jessie thought again about those initials and what they might mean.

It was like a math equation with symbols:

if

   M.M. = Megan Moriarty

and

   E.T. = Evan Treski

and

   a heart = love,

then

   M.M. + E.T. inside a heart =

   Megan Moriarty loves Evan Treski.

But what did *that* mean?

Jessie decided to go straight to the primary source.

Chapter 5
Love Stuff

assonance (n) a poetic technique in which the middle sound of a word (usually a vowel) is repeated in words that are next to the word or near it, such as *silly little chimps*

Evan was grabbing a plastic spoon at the utensil table in the cafeteria when he saw Jessie walk up to Megan, who was near the front of the line. It was noisy in the cafeteria, the way it usually was, but Evan was close enough to hear Jessie's voice, which was always loud and clear.

"Do you love Evan?"

Evan's head snapped in the direction of Jessie's voice. He saw Megan's back stiffen and her face turn bright red. The dozen or so kids closest in line straightened up and turned their full attention to Jessie and Megan. Tessa squealed, her hands flying to her mouth. Scott Spencer started laughing, and several of the boys erupted in a chorus of "Oooh."

Evan felt his face flame and his stomach drop. He wanted to run out of the cafeteria.

Salley Knight, who was standing right behind Megan, said, "You're not supposed to say something like that!"

"Why not?" Jessie asked, still talking in her usual loud way.

"Because . . ." Salley threw her hands up, shaking her head.

Evan walked quickly back to his assigned seat at his lunch table, careful to keep his eyes down. The kids at the table hadn't heard what Jessie had said, but by the end of lunch, the news had traveled up and down the aisles. There were lots of jokes about kissing. Malik turned two soggy french fries into lips and squeezed them open and closed while making loud smooching noises. A bunch of girls started to sing "My Heart Will Go On," so loudly that the cafeteria ladies told the whole class that they were the worst group of the day and were in danger of losing recess. Even that didn't stop the snickering and poking. Evan wished the floor would swallow him whole.

When the doors to the playground were finally opened and the horde of noisy fourth-graders ran outside, Evan stayed behind and cornered Jessie at the trash can.

"What are you doing? How come you said that?" He wanted to shake her, as if that would make her understand what she'd done.

"Said what?" asked Jessie.

Evan dropped his voice to a dangerous whisper. "That Megan and me are in love."

"I did *not* say that!"

"Well, that's what everyone is saying now. What's with you, Jess? Come on! Even you—"

"All I did was ask a simple question. All I did was ask Megan if she loves you because that's what it says in the girls' bathroom."

Evan felt his stomach drop to his knees for the second time that day. He tried to ask Jessie what she meant, but it was as if he'd forgotten how his tongue worked. It just lay there in his mouth, unable to form words.

"C'mon! Line up!" shouted one of the cafeteria ladies to the last few stragglers busing their trays and throwing out their trash.

Evan placed both hands on Jessie's shoulders and bent his head down close to hers. In a whisper, he asked, "What does it say in the girls' bathroom?"

Jessie put her hands together, both thumbs meeting in a downward-facing point to form a perfect heart. "M.M. plus E.T.," she said.

Evan felt another wave of heat rise up from his shirt collar. The noise of the cafeteria swirled around him.

"Did Megan write that . . . that thing in the bathroom?" Evan asked.

"No. I don't think so. I don't know! How am I supposed to know?"

"Can you find out?"

"Why?" asked Jessie. "What is it with all this love stuff?"

Evan again had the feeling of wanting to shake Jessie. Why didn't she understand things that everyone else did? "Just find out, would ya? Ask her. And then tell me. But don't tell her I asked you to find out. And don't tell *anyone* else. Swear it!"

Evan headed for the playground, wanting to shake off this almost-sick feeling. He pushed open the door and shouted, "Hey!" as Ryan ran by on the blacktop. "Wait for me!"

He could count on Jessie to find out the answer, but how long would that take? Valentine's Day was just four days away, and Evan needed answers.

Chapter 6
Exclusive

exclusive (n) a story that is reported by only one newspaper because that newspaper is the only one with the information

Jessie walked home alone that afternoon. It was hard work being around other people, particularly kids in her grade. There were so many things to figure out. She had to watch their faces closely and listen hard to the *way* they talked. Did their eyes open wide? Did they look down at the ground? Did they whisper? Or get loud? It was like trying to solve a math problem that never ended.

Take, for example, what had happened on the playground after lunch.

After promising Evan to find out who drew the heart on the bathroom wall, Jessie had wandered outside in search of Megan.

She found her at the swings, but when Jessie came close, Megan walked away. Jessie tried to follow her, but Megan kept moving, first to the monkey bars and then the slide and then the picnic tables.

Finally, Salley came up to Jessie and said, "Megan told me to tell you that she doesn't want to talk to you right now because she's really mad and she doesn't want to say something she'll regret later."

"Why is she mad?" asked Jessie. "I just asked a question."

Salley shook her head and said, "You're not supposed to ask about stuff like that. Not out loud where everyone can hear you. No one says that stuff out loud. Obviously. You only talk about it late at night at a slumber party after all the lights are out and everyone's half asleep."

But Jessie had never been to a slumber party, so she didn't know about that.

"Why? Is it some kind of secret?"

Salley looked at her sideways, clearly puzzled.

"Well, yeah. That's why everyone's so interested. Everyone wants to know who likes who."

"Everyone?" said Jessie. "Does everyone like someone?"

"Pretty much," said Salley. "I mean, it's fourth grade. We're not little kids anymore."

But Jessie didn't understand what it meant to like someone in *that* way. And when she tried to smile and wave at Megan from across the playground—which she *knew* was the right way to tell someone "I want to be friends with you"—Megan wouldn't look at her.

Walking home after school, Jessie got to thinking. If what Salley said was true—that everyone liked someone and it was all a big secret—then *here* was a hot topic that 4-O was interested in. She would need to collect data, of course. In just four days! But when she did, she would have a newspaper article that everyone would want to read.

Jessie imagined the headline of her front-page story:

Who Likes Who—A 4-O Forum Exclusive!

Chapter 7
Proud Words

slant rhyme (n) two words that have the same final consonant sound (such as "stopped" and "wept") or two words with the same middle vowel sound (such as "barn" and "yard"). They sound almost like rhyming words, but not quite.

The plan had been to go to Ryan's house and shoot hoops, but then Evan suggested they walk uptown to get slices of pizza. So they'd all called their mothers using the school office phone, and now they were walking up the hill to Town House, which didn't have the best pizza in town, but it was the closest.

Evan was dribbling the ball as they walked, and the bounce of the ball seemed to keep time to the words that kept drumming in his head: "nudgers and shovers in spite of ourselves." The words made a steady beat that sounded right with the pounding of the basketball on the frozen pavement. And "nudgers" and "shovers" together was an example of slant rhyme, which Evan thought was pretty neat.

Just as they reached the door of the pizza shop, Ryan said, "Hey, look!" and elbowed Evan so hard that Evan half stumbled in mid-dribble. When he looked up, he saw Megan and her mom walking right toward them. The ball bounced out of his reach and went rolling into the street. There was a lot of afternoon traffic, and several cars had to jam on their brakes to avoid running over the ball. Evan waited until everyone had stopped and then sprinted across the street to grab the ball, angry at it the way a mother would be mad at a kid for running into the street without first looking both ways. Mostly, though, he was embarrassed. Embarrassed to be making such a scene in the middle of town, embarrassed that he'd flubbed his dribble in front of Megan, and embarrassed that his friends had seen the whole thing.

When he got back to the curb, Megan and her mom were gone, but Paul and Ryan were laughing so hard, they'd sat down on the bench outside of Town House. Adam wasn't laughing, but he hadn't offered to help Evan, either.

"Oooh, Megan!" said Paul, clasping his hands and pressing them to his heart. "I love you! I love you! I love you! Ooops! I dropped my basketball. Excuse me!"

"No, no, it's like this," said Ryan, who could barely get the words out of his mouth because he was laughing so much. "Oh, Megan! When you're around, my hands turn to Jell-O!" and he started jiggling his hands in the air.

"Just shut up, would you?" said Evan, and he pulled back the arm that was loaded with the basketball and looked like he might fire it right at their heads.

"Come on," said Adam, pulling open the pizza shop door. "You're acting like a bunch of idiots."

"What's with him?" Paul muttered to Ryan as they followed Adam inside. Evan brought up the rear, the basketball pressed against his hip, wishing he'd never suggested going uptown that afternoon.

After they'd finished their pizza slices and decided it was too cold to play basketball, they all went home. Evan climbed the stairs to his bedroom, hung the Locked sign on his door, then closed it firmly and pushed the edge of his desk in front of it so there was no way anyone could "accidentally" come in. He sat down and pulled out the stack of Post-it notes from his top drawer. It was easy to come up with the first six words. He'd been thinking about them on the walk home.

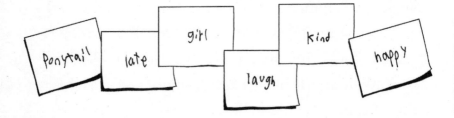

But after that, he couldn't think of what to do.

He heard Jessie's door open, and then came the sound he dreaded: her impatient knocking at his door. Sometimes he wondered whether there was some kind of magnetic force field around the Locked sign. Every time he hung it up, Jessie appeared immediately.

"Busy. Can't talk right now," Evan called through the door.

"I need you to look at something." Jessie's voice was matter-of-fact. Evan couldn't tell if she had even heard him.

"I said I'm busy. Come back later."

"But later is too late. I need you to look at something *now*."

"Not now. And not later, if you keep bugging me!"

"But what are you *doing*?" Evan could hear her knocking her shoe against the jamb of the door.

Evan buried his head in his hands. "I'm *thinking*."

"Thinking about what?"

Evan slammed a book down over the Post-it notes, pushed the desk roughly away from the door, and flung the door open. "Why are you always such a pest?" he shouted.

"I'm not *always* a pest," she said. "Just when I really need something." She held up a single piece of paper in her hand. "Can you look at this and tell me if it's good?"

"No! I really can't. That's why I said later. Because later means later, Jess. You've gotta learn that!" Evan retreated back into his room and slammed the door shut. He heard Jessie's voice from the other side.

"Your sign flipped around. Do you want me to fix it for you?"

"Yes!" said Evan.

There was a slight scraping noise, and then Jessie said quietly, "Okay, I did it."

"Thanks," said Evan tightly, sitting back down at his desk.

And it was funny, because something about the interruption or yelling or maybe just getting up from his desk and moving around suddenly made it easy for Evan to fill his entire desk with Post-it note words.

He started moving the words around. He tore one word in half.

He lumped together all the words that started with *f.*

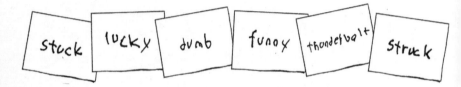

He gathered up the short *u* sounds.

Then he grouped the long *i* sounds.

flying   Kind   I   Smile

He added more words and tossed out others. Half an hour later, he leaned back in his chair and looked at the poem on his desk.

Pony girl
flying by
always late
lately in my heart
you laugh your
happy laugh
you smile your
kindly smile
you gallop past
me standing still
dumb struck

He liked it. He felt proud of the words on the page.

From his top desk drawer, he pulled out a piece of paper and quickly copied the poem over. He was worried Jessie would come knocking again before he finished. But when he was done, he noticed that in his haste he'd misspelled three words. When he tried to fix them, his poem looked like a mess.

He took another piece of paper from his desk drawer and copied the whole poem over again, slowly and neatly, in his best handwriting. Then he put the good copy in his desk drawer, buried under several notebooks and old copies of *Mad* magazine, and crumpled up the messy draft and threw it in his trash can.

Chapter 8
Survey

survey (n) a series of questions that investigates the opinions or experiences of a group of people

Jessie was irritated. The color photocopier in her mom's office wasn't working. At least, it wasn't printing color copies. A yellow light blinked, telling her that one of the color ink tanks was empty.

To Jessie, this was a tragedy. The wings of the butterflies were supposed to be bright blue. The hearts were meant to be red. The delicate centers of the daisies were colored a buttery yellow.

In disgust, she punched the "copy" button and printed out twenty-seven copies of her survey in boring black and white.

Then she packed the special survey box she'd made into her backpack and walked out the door.

On the playground, she stayed apart from the others, waiting for the bell that would signal it was time to line up. Megan, of course, was late as usual, and Jessie didn't know if the other girls were mad at her, too. She decided not to ask them. Evan had explained this to her: asking people if they were mad at you sometimes made them even madder.

Jessie wasn't the only one keeping to herself that morning. David Kirkorian was also on his own, wandering along the edge of the playground, picking up rocks, and talking to himself. Eventually, he worked his way around to where Jessie was standing, waiting for the bell.

"What's that?" he asked, pointing at the stack of papers that Jessie held to her chest.

"Nothing," said Jessie.

"It can't be nothing," said David. "Just say 'None ya' if you don't want to talk about it."

"Okay, none ya."

"Why?" asked David. "Is it a secret?"

Jessie thought about that. It *wasn't* a secret. But it was *about* a secret, or really a whole lot of secrets. Jessie had that uncomfortable feeling that she was about to mess around in something she didn't really understand. Maybe David could help her figure it out.

"Well, it's a survey. A bunch of questions. Everyone in the class fills one out—*anonymously*—and then I add everything up and hand out the results. In my newspaper. It's going to be the front-page story."

"A survey about what?" He seemed really interested, and Jessie felt encouraged. Maybe this *was* a good idea.

"Love," she said. "The survey asks if the person likes anyone, you know, *like*-likes. *Anonymously.* Obviously, no one's going to say out loud if they like someone else." She looked at David closely to see if he agreed with this statement.

"Obviously," he said, looking up at the sky.

"And then there are some other questions, too. You want to see?"

Survey

1. Do you have a crush on someone?

2. Is it someone in 4-O?

3. Does the person know you have a crush on them?

4. What's the best way to tell someone you have a crush on them? (circle one)
   - tell them yourself
   - ask a friend to tell them
   - write a note
   - other (please specify _____)

write the name of the person you have a crush on:

_____

(hint: disguise your handwriting)

"Sure," said David, but he shrugged one shoulder casually as if to say that he didn't think the topic was really worth talking about.

Still, when she handed him the top sheet from her stack, he readjusted his glasses and started to read with lightning speed. When he got to the bottom of the page, his eyes went right back to the top and started reading again.

"Mrs. Overton is never going to let you pass this out," said David, giving the sheet back to Jessie as if it were a losing hand in gin rummy.

"I'm going to convince her," said Jessie. "It's my extra credit project for math: finding practical ways to use decimals. She can't argue with that."

"Yes, she can," said David, his lip curling just a little at one end. "She's the teacher. She can do whatever she wants."

This was so true! Teachers did get to do whatever they wanted. Still, Mrs. Overton was pretty fair. Fairer than most. She *couldn't* say no to a project that involved the whole class *and* decimals. Could she? Jessie was even planning to make a pie chart once she had collected the data. A pie chart! Mrs. Overton loved pie charts almost as much as she loved poems.

But when they trooped into the classroom to begin the day, Mrs. Overton wasn't there. Instead, Mrs. Feeney was sitting behind Mrs. Overton's desk, and the hearts of all the kids sank. Mrs. Feeney was, by far, the worst substitute teacher. She was old and sour and hardly paid any attention to what was going on in the classroom. She also sent more kids to Mrs. Fletcher's office than all the other substitute teachers combined. Jessie couldn't figure out why the school kept hiring her. It must be because she was available at a moment's notice.

"Settle down," bellowed Mrs. Feeney as the students walked into the classroom. *We're not even making any noise!* thought Jessie. She took her chair down from her desk, then walked up to Mrs. Feeney with her survey held tightly to her chest. For some strange reason, David walked up right behind her.

"Mrs. Feeney, I have something I need to pass out to all the kids." She held up the stack of papers, but didn't turn them around.

"What is it?" Just then the ding-a-ling of a cell phone was heard coming from behind Mrs. Overton's desk. Mrs. Feeney immediately moved to retrieve her phone from her enormous handbag.

"An extra credit project," said David. "For math."

"How long will it take?" Mrs. Feeney's eyes were on her phone, reading the screen. "Oh, for Pete's sake!" She poked at the phone a few times, but this didn't seem to improve her mood.

"Less than five minutes. And I guarantee everyone will be quiet and stay in their seats the whole time!"

"All right. Be quick. I need to take this call. But I am *right outside in the hallway,* so no monkey business. And don't think I don't mean it." She sailed out into the hallway, with the phone already at her ear, and closed the door behind her.

Jessie looked at David, who looked right back at her. Their eyes seemed to say, *That was just too easy.*

"Okay, everybody listen up," said Jessie in her best in-charge voice. "I'm doing an extra credit project—"

"Dweeb!" shouted Paul, but he said it jokingly. During the course of the year, the kids in 4-O had gotten used to Jessie. Sometimes she was a bossy pain in the neck, but at other times she had good ideas. Different ideas. Like the time she got the whole class to create a courtroom on the playground, complete with a judge and jury and verdict. Jessie was almost never boring.

"It's a survey," she said, ignoring Paul. "And *everyone* has to fill one out. But don't write your name, and when you're done, fold your paper up a bunch of times and put it in this special box." Jessie showed them a shoebox with the lid taped on and a thin slot cut into the top. Once a paper went through the slot, there would be no way to get it out without cutting through the cardboard.

While she was talking, Jessie was handing out the papers, one on each desk, face-down. Tessa was the first to talk.

"I'm not answering this!"

"Me, neither," said Paul.

Megan raised her hand. "This is kind of private stuff."

Jessie stared at her and tried to figure out whether Megan was still mad. Then she looked around the room. A lot of kids were shifting uncomfortably in their seats. No one had written a single thing on the survey. Why were they against this? It was just a survey, and it was anonymous. Jessie couldn't see what the big deal was.

She looked at Evan. He was leaning over the top of his desk, his head resting in his hand, staring at her. He gave just a little shake of his head, as if to say, *What are you doing now, Jess?*

Then David said, "Don't you want to know?"

"Know what?" asked Ryan.

"Know what everyone else is thinking? About boys and girls and love?"

That got most of the class laughing and calling out.

"Love!" hooted Scott Spencer, slapping his desk. "Oooh, lo-o-o-o-ve!"

"What's so funny about love?" asked Megan. "Love is a good thing."

"Yeah," said Salley. "Everybody should love everybody."

"I don't love anyone," said Christopher, "and no one can make me."

"So, what's the big deal?" asked Jessie. "Just write that down in the survey and hand it in."

"No way. What if I'm like . . . you know . . . the only one?" He looked around the classroom, and his eyes got big and he wasn't laughing anymore.

The class grew quiet when he said that. It was as if each kid was thinking the same thing: *Am I the only one?*

David broke the silence. "So—don't you want to know?"

"It'll only take a couple of seconds," said Jessie. "But we've got to be quick because Mrs. Feeney is going to come back any minute, and I guarantee you she won't let us do this survey."

If there was one thing that united the kids in 4-O at that moment, it was their dislike of Mrs. Feeney.

"Just do it," said Megan, and she began to fill in her survey.

"Yeah," said Evan. "Do it."

Everyone started writing, and then a competition broke out over who could fold the paper the most number of times. (Six was the best any-one could manage.) Jessie quickly filled out a survey herself. Her answers were easy: "no," "no," "no idea." She stuffed hers in the box along with everyone else's.

"Hurry up!" said several of the kids as Maddy Garber, the last one, slid her paper into the sealed-up shoebox.

Jessie pressed the shoebox to her chest. "I solemnly promise that I will guard this box *with my life* for the rest of the day. I will keep it with me at all times, and I will report the results to you on Monday, Valentine's Day."

"She's coming!" shouted Jack, who had peeked through the glass of the door after sharpening his pencil.

Mrs. Feeney walked in and found the entire class of 4-O seated silently at their desks, all eyes staring at her expectantly.

"Well, I guess we can get started now," she said, as if she'd been waiting for *them* instead of the other way around. "Hopefully Mrs. Overton will be back after lunch. She had to take her cat to the vet."

"Langston?" asked Megan, looking around at the other kids in her desk group. Several kids started to talk, and Jessie's eyes couldn't help jumping to the laminated photo of Langston over the door with a speech bubble coming out of his mouth that read BE KIND AND DO YOUR WORK!

"Quiet!" barked Mrs. Feeney. "Some kind of an emergency, I guess. There's no lesson plan, I know that." She stared glumly at Mrs. Overton's neat desk.

Oh, brother, thought Jessie. Mrs. Feeney practically needed to be dragged through the day. "We start with Morning Meeting," she said.

"And then the Poem of the Day," added Evan. Jessie frowned. She'd been hoping they could just skip that and get right to math.

"Poetry?" said Mrs. Feeney, raising her eyebrows. "Well, I don't know anything about poetry."

"It's okay," said Megan. "We'll teach you."

The class moved, fairly quietly, to the rug area and sat on the floor.

After Morning Meeting, Salley turned the page on the easel to reveal the Poem of the Day. Mrs. Feeney called on Ray to read the poem out loud.

TOAD
by Valerie Worth

When the flowers
Turned clever, and
Earned wide
Tender red petals
For themselves,

When the birds
Learned about feathers,
Spread green tails,
Grew cockades
On their heads,

The toad said:
Someone has got
To remember
The mud, and
I'm not proud.

There was silence. Mrs. Overton had taught them
to let a poem sink in before talking about it. But Mrs.

83

Feeney didn't know about that, so she was the first to comment. "You see. That's what I mean. It doesn't make any sense to me. I'm just not a poetry person."

Well, Jessie wasn't a poetry person, either, but she thought it was pretty weak of Mrs. Feeney to just give up without even trying. She looked at Evan. He was reading the poem again to himself, his lips moving silently, shaping the strange words.

Megan raised her hand. "The flowers are kind of selfish," she said. "They're just thinking about themselves."

"What's a cockade?" asked Christopher.

"I have no idea," said Mrs. Feeney. She didn't move from her seat.

"We have a dictionary, you know," said Jessie.

"Well, feel free to look it up, if you want," said Mrs. Feeney.

Jessie stood up, exasperated, as Evan raised his hand and asked, "Why does someone have to remember the mud?" Jessie noticed he wasn't directing his question at Mrs. Feeney. He was looking at the other kids in 4-O.

Salley answered. "Because mud is one of the things you take for granted. No one bothers to *remember* it. But it's important. At least to a toad."

"Toads love mud!" said Malik.

"Hey, it's a love poem!" said Tessa. "A love poem for mud." And instead of laughing, the kids in 4-O nodded their heads and agreed. It turns out you could even write a love poem about mud.

"A cockade is a fancy thing you wear on your hat to show that you're better than everyone else," said Jessie, her finger still marking the spot in the dictionary—the *grown-up* dictionary—that Mrs. Overton kept on the shelf beside her desk. "It's a sign of rank." She looked particularly at Mrs. Feeney, but Mrs. Feeney didn't seem to be listening. She had her eye on the clock.

At recess, Jessie carried the box of surveys with her to the playground and guarded it safely. Three more days until Valentine's Day. Tomorrow, Saturday, and Sunday. Only three days to calculate the results of the survey and write her article. Kids kept wandering over to her on the playground. It was as if they were ants drawn to a big sticky spot of spilled lemonade on the sidewalk. They couldn't keep away.

But as soon as the class went back inside, they forgot all about the surveys. There was something much more interesting on their desks: more candy hearts! And the messages on these were just as personal as the other ones.

"Mine says SMART GUY," said David, waving his box in the air.

"Hey, look!" said Taffy Morgan. "Mine says TWINKLE TOES," and she held up one foot to show the glittery shoes she was wearing that day.

Jessie's hearts said GO-GETTER on them. It was as if the hearts were telling her to spring into action now that there was something to investigate!

Obviously, Mrs. Overton hadn't put these candy hearts on their desks. So who had? Jessie whipped out her reporter's notebook and began to write down the names of everyone in the classroom and the messages on their hearts. As she made her list, she wondered: *Will there be more hearts tomorrow?*

David: SMART GUY

Taffy: TWINKLE TOES

Tessa: NICE SMILE

Ryan: SLAM DUNK

Sally: KIND KID

Tessie: GO-GETTER

Adam: GERBIL CATCHER

Megan: B-BALL PRO

Michael: WORLD TRAVELER

Christopher: BALONEY KING

Malik: THE JOKER

Nina: SPELLING CHAMP

Mrs. Feeney didn't know the new rule about no candy in the classroom, but she did know her old rule about no noise in the classroom, and she promptly threatened to send all of them to the principal's office if they didn't "pipe down and put a cork in it." She handed out math worksheets and said the first person to make a sound would miss lunch recess. Jessie thought that sounded pretty good. She'd rather stay inside where it was warm and work on her newspaper than go out on the playground and guard the survey box. So as soon as she finished the problems on the page, she got up to sharpen her pencil, but wandered over to Evan's desk. He was hunched over his math paper with a scowl on his face.

"What do your hearts say?" Jessie whispered, pointing to the box that sat on the corner of his desk. The box was open and a couple of hearts had spilled out.

"Nothing," he muttered. He grabbed the box and tried to scoop up the two stray hearts, but accidentally knocked one to the floor. Jessie stooped down to pick it up, and before she handed it back to Evan, she quickly read what it said.

Chapter 9
Love Comes in All Shapes and Sizes

cliché (n) an overused expression that lacks power because it is so familiar; for example: "as bright as a penny" or "love comes in all shapes and sizes" or "one smart cookie"

After school, the guys wouldn't stop teasing Evan about being in love with Megan.

"I am not in love with Megan Moriarty!" he shouted at them as he pedaled his bike away from the playground, furious and embarrassed. Suddenly he felt that there were so many things he was ashamed of. He was ashamed that he liked Megan. He was ashamed that he liked poetry.

And he was ashamed that he was the only one in the class who got store-bought candy hearts when everyone else got special messages written just for them.

When it had happened the first time on Monday, he hadn't thought much about it. Candy was candy. Who cared if his hearts just said FOR YOU? But now it seemed as if whoever was giving out the candy was purposely pointing out that he was not very special. It made him feel the way he did when his grandmother forgot him but remembered everybody else.

On the way home, he rode right by Megan, and he didn't even say hello. He rode fast, as if he didn't see her right there on the sidewalk looking at him, one hand raised and smiling.

And why didn't Jessie know whether Megan had drawn the heart in the girls' bathroom? How hard was it to find that out?

"Just ask her, for Pete's sake," he'd said to Jessie in the hallway after recess.

But Jessie had waved the taped-up survey box in his face and said, "I'm a little busy, you know!"

He decided to loop the long way home so that he could pedal out some of his frustration. More than anything else, he wished he had basketball practice that afternoon. But it was Thursday, so no practice. By the time he got home, Jessie was already there. They walked through the front door together and found Mrs. Treski in the kitchen, pouring hot water from the kettle into a mug.

"Grab the mail, will you?" she said, so Evan doubled back and pulled a stack of letters and catalogs out of the mailbox by the front door.

"I've got stuff to do," said Jessie, heading straight for the stairs. "No interruptions!"

"Yeah, right," said Evan, dropping the letters on the kitchen counter.

"What's that about?" asked Mrs. Treski, flipping through the mail.

"Just some extra credit project she's doing," said Evan glumly.

"Hmm. That's Jessie. Hey, look. Here's something for you." She held up a small square envelope with red lettering on it. Evan's heart did a 360 back-flip. Had Megan sent him a valentine? Should he open it in front of his mother? Did he even want it?

His mom held up another envelope that looked exactly the same. "And here's one for Jessie." She looked puzzled. "I wonder why . . ."

Evan tore open the envelope, not sure what he hoped to find inside. It was a card with a picture of Snoopy hugging Woodstock, and the message inside read, "Love comes in all shapes and sizes."

"It's from Grandma," he said.

"I know. I could tell from the handwriting."

"Look what she wrote," said Evan, holding out the card. "Dear Evan, I love you and miss you and think of you every day. Hope you have a great Valentine's Day. See you soon! Love, Grandma."

Evan looked at his mom, and they both started to laugh. It was hard not to, living with Grandma. Her brain worked in crazy ways these days. Sometimes she thought she was twenty years old. Sometimes she forgot she lived in the same house with the Treskis. Sometimes she didn't even remember who they were. And sometimes she was just fine.

Evan went to the cupboard and got down everything he needed to make hot chocolate: a mug, a spoon, hot chocolate mix, and mini-marshmallows. As he scooped the mix into his cup, his thoughts returned to the gloom that hung over him on the bike ride home. And that made him think of other things, too, and so he asked his mother, "Did *you* get a valentine?"

Mrs. Treski laughed. "Now, who would send me a valentine?"

"I don't know," said Evan, stirring the hot water and chocolate mix in his cup. "Maybe . . . Dad?"

His mom took a sip of her tea and looked at him closely. "No. No valentine from Dad. Were you hoping I'd get one from him?"

Evan shrugged, watching the billows of steam rising from his stirring spoon. "Well, you were married, right?"

"Yep," said Mrs. Treski. "We were."

"So . . ." Evan dropped a fistful of mini-marshmallows into his cup. His mother opened her mouth as if she was going to say something about that, but then she closed it again. "How does that work?" asked Evan. "How can you be in love and then not in love anymore?"

"You know, I'm not sure about that myself."

"Maybe it was never love? Maybe you just made a mistake."

"No, it was definitely love. Believe me. For both of us. But—it didn't last. Sometimes love doesn't."

Evan shook his head. "All the poems make it sound like love is forever. It's bigger than anything and the most important thing in the world. But if it can just go like *that* . . . just disappear . . ." Evan threw his hand up as if he was tossing a piece of trash over his shoulder.

Evan's mother paused. "It didn't just go, Evan. It put up a fight. A big, long fight. Do you remember? Were you old enough?"

Evan nodded, then took a short, hot sip of his drink. "I remember the fighting."

"That was love. That was love doing everything it could to hang in there. But in the end, it couldn't. So Dad and I decided to be apart. But I'll always love your father."

"You say that! You always say that," said Evan. "But what does it mean if you're not married anymore?"

"It means it's a different kind of love. There are all kinds in the world, you know."

"Mrs. O. says that, too. She says you can love a song or a forest or a friend or a—you know—a person, a person you're 'in love' with." Evan buried his face in the hot steam rising from his cup so his mother wouldn't see his eyes.

"Mrs. Overton is one smart cookie."

Evan nodded, still keeping his face tilted down. Love was confusing.

"Hey, Mom. I wrote a poem. About Grandma. Do you want to read it?"

"Sure," she said. "Bring it on."

He dug through his backpack until he found the folded-up piece of paper he'd stuck in the back pocket of his binder. He handed it to his mom, wondering why his heart was beating hard, so hard he thought it was going to knock itself right out of his chest.

Mrs. Treski read the poem once. Then she put the paper down on the counter, smoothing over the page with her hand, and read it again. She looked up at Evan, and Evan stopped breathing. It was as if everything inside him stopped—his heart and his lungs and his brain—just stopped. In that instant, he would have given anything to have his poem back, safe and hidden in his binder, where no one would know that it even existed. It was just too hard, having it out there in the world for everyone to see.

"That is the most remarkable poem I've ever read in my entire life, Evan," said his mother. Her voice was quiet, as if she'd just discovered a new planet or found a rare bird on her front lawn.

Evan's heart suddenly flooded his whole system with too much blood; it rushed past his ears with a whooshing noise that made it hard to hear. "You think it's good?" he asked.

"You have a talent," she said, tapping the page. "A rare talent." She shook her head. "I didn't know you like poetry."

"I didn't either," he said. "But I do." Evan couldn't believe he'd just said that out loud. He'd actually admitted to liking poetry. *Next thing you know, I'll start saying that I like Megan Moriarty out loud!* His ears pinked up at the thought.

There was a crash followed by a thud from upstairs, then Jessie yelled down, "I'm okay. I just tripped."

Evan and his mom laughed. Jessie was kind of like Old Faithful, that geyser at Yellowstone Park that Evan had studied in third grade. She could be counted on to blow every few hours.

"I've got a picture frame you can have," said Mrs. Treski, handing the poem back to Evan. "You could copy the poem over and frame it and then give it as a Valentine's gift to Grandma. I bet she'd really like it."

Evan thought of his poem on display for everyone to see. *Everyone.* It made him feel both proud and nervous, both excited and a little sick to his stomach. "Maybe," he said.

Evan walked upstairs slowly, looking down at the poem in his hand. It didn't feel so bad admitting he liked poetry. Maybe he'd show one or two of his poems to Mrs. Overton. Maybe he'd even show one of them to his friends. Not this one. A different one. Maybe. But he would never, ever admit that he liked Megan. He'd rather die than have his friends know that.

He walked into his room, but before he even had a chance to close the door behind him, he noticed that some of the trash from his wastebasket was spilled onto the floor.

Chapter 10
Snooping

snooping (v.) investigating or searching in a secretive way to uncover private information

It had been an accident. Really and truly. The only reason Jessie had gone into Evan's room in the first place was that she'd needed a piece of paper. That's all. She wasn't looking for anything else. She wasn't snooping. She *wasn't.*

And even though she wasn't supposed to go in Evan's room without asking, and she definitely wasn't allowed to look in his top desk drawer without permission, she was in a big hurry to count up the results of the survey. And Evan was *all* the way downstairs. And he'd been in such a bad mood when they'd walked in the front door together. And she was in a big hurry. That was the thing. She didn't have time to follow *all* the rules.

But when she grabbed a piece of paper out of Evan's desk drawer and turned to run back out the door—so fast it was as if she hadn't even broken the rule in the first place—she tripped over Evan's wastebasket, which crashed into the floor lamp, and the papers spilled all over the floor. They were like little animals escaping from their cage. The wastebasket was made of wire, just like a cage, and Jessie couldn't help imagining the papers shouting, "Free! We're free! At last, we're free!"

"I'm okay! I just tripped!" she shouted so that Evan and their mother wouldn't come running upstairs to see what the noise was.

She started to scoop up the crumpled-up pieces of paper, still thinking about the animals escaping from their cage, and then one of them really did look like a turtle. *Look at that,* she thought. There was the shell and a leg and a head poking out. Jessie was good at noticing patterns and shapes, and this crumpled-up piece of paper definitely looked like a turtle.

She picked up the piece of paper, tugged on the head, and then pushed on it to see if she could imitate the way a turtle pokes its head out of its shell and then pulls it in when it's threatened. And that's when the paper became uncrumpled and she saw a few of the words on the page.

Words were meant to be read. Everyone knew that! You didn't write a word down on a piece of paper if you didn't expect someone to read it. Otherwise you would just leave that word in your head.

So without really thinking and almost before she knew that she was doing it, Jessie uncrumpled the paper and spread it out in front of her. And then, when she got that feeling in her stomach—that tingle that told her she might be doing something wrong— it was too late, because a question had popped into her mind. And once that happened, there was no stopping Jessie. She needed to know the answer to the question, just as she had needed to know the answers to all the other questions that had come up

Pony girl
flying by
always late
lately in my heart
you laugh your
happy laugh
you smile your
kindly smile
you gallop past
me standing still
dumb   struck

this year: Who stole the lemonade money? How did Scott Spencer buy an Xbox 20/20? Where did the New Year's Eve bell go? What was wrong with Maxwell? The questions were like math problems, and Jessie couldn't rest until the equation was solved.

Who was *pony girl*? What did these words mean?

Jessie heard a sound from downstairs. She wasn't sure what it was, but it reminded her that she was in Evan's room without having asked him for permission. So she scooped the balls of paper on the floor into the trash can, set the trash can upright, then ran out of Evan's room.

Back in her own room with the door closed, she settled down at her desk and smoothed the wrinkled paper in front of her. A thought flickered through her mind: *Am I stealing something by taking the paper?* But no, that didn't make sense. The paper was trash, and you couldn't steal trash. Besides, Jessie carried the trash out of Evan's room every week. It was one of her household chores. What was the difference between carrying it out today and carrying it out on Saturday?

Still, she opened her door and hung up the Locked sign, then closed her door again and slipped the paper into her top desk drawer. There was no time to think about trash or words or Evan. Right now, she had to tally up the responses to her survey.

Using a pair of scissors, she carefully cut the top off the shoebox and dumped all the surveys onto her bed. Half of them were folded so many times, they looked like square paper rocks. A few of them even rolled off the bed and onto the floor. Jessie carefully unfolded each survey and spread it out on her bed. By the time she'd finished, the entire bed was covered in paper.

But when she counted up the surveys, there were only twenty-six. She looked on the floor and double-checked her backpack but couldn't find the twenty-seventh survey.

How was that possible? No one had been absent today; she was sure of it. Maybe someone had not handed one in? She wondered who it was.

Jessie was still staring at her bed when she heard Evan climbing the stairs and then *bang, bang, bang,* on her door.

"I'm busy," she said.

"Open up!" he commanded. "Now."

Jessie didn't like the sound of that.

She opened her door a tiny crack, then pressed her face up to the thin slice of the opening. The surveys were spread out on her bed, and she didn't want anyone to see them.

"You can't come in," said Jessie, her lips pressed against the narrow space of the open door.

"I don't want to," said Evan. "Did you come in my room?"

"Yes," said Jessie. "But only for a second."

"It doesn't matter. You're not allowed in my room without my permission. You owe me a dollar."

Jessie knew there was no way out of this one. A rule is a rule. "Okay," she said. "I'll pay the dumb fine."

"It's not dumb. You wouldn't think it was dumb if

I came in your room." But Evan never came to Jessie's room anymore. Jessie wished he would sometimes. Especially if it meant he had to pay her a dollar.

Evan stood waiting at the door.

"Now, you mean?" asked Jessie. "You want the dollar now?"

"Yes." Evan didn't move. His face looked like it was carved out of granite.

"Oh, fine," said Jessie. She closed the door and went to get her lock box from its hiding place behind some books on the top shelf of her bookcase. Then she retrieved the key, which was hanging on a small nail that she had tapped into the doorjamb inside her closet. She did all this very quietly, as if she were a spy on a secret mission, so that if Evan was listening at the door, he wouldn't be able to figure out her secret hiding places.

She opened the door again, just a sliver, and handed Evan the dollar through the narrow crack. She hated giving up money, especially when she didn't get anything in return.

"Why'd you come in my room anyway?" asked Evan.

"I needed a piece of paper."

Evan's eyes narrowed to two dark slits. "You mean you went in my desk drawer?"

"Only for a split second!" said Jessie. "I just needed *one piece of paper.*" She said the last part as if she was pleading for her life.

"You owe me another dollar!" shouted Evan.

"I do not!"

"Do, too! It's bad enough you went in my room. Now you're snooping around in my desk!"

"I wasn't snooping," said Jessie and meant it with all her heart. She had just wanted a piece of paper. Why did everything have to turn into such a big deal?

"I'm not leaving until you pay me another dollar. And that's the rule from now on."

"Oh, fine," said Jessie. She was starting to get that sick feeling in her stomach when she sensed that something was going wrong but she couldn't figure out exactly what. Was Evan going to ask her about tipping over the wastebasket? Jessie didn't want to talk about that, even though she didn't think she'd done anything wrong.

When she handed Evan the second dollar, he still didn't look pleased. How could anyone who had just gotten two dollars for nothing not be happy?

"You have to clean up the mess you made, too," said Evan. "You left trash on the floor."

Jessie closed the door behind her with a defiant slam, then walked across the hall. She was just about to cross the threshold to Evan's room when she froze in midstep. "Wait a minute," she said. "Is this a trick?" It was just the kind of trick she would have thought of to earn an easy dollar.

"No, for Pete's sake!" Evan said. "You have permission to go into my room to clean up the mess!"

There were two scraps of paper on the floor, and Jessie was kicking herself for not having noticed them before. Evan watched her pick up the papers and throw them in his trash can. He still had that look on his face. The one that Jessie couldn't quite figure out. Was it anger? Frustration? Impatience?

Suspicion? Maybe Evan was having mixed-up feelings, in which case Jessie knew she couldn't figure them out. One feeling was hard enough to decipher; a whole bunch of them left her completely confused.

When she walked past him on her way back to her room, Evan grabbed her elbow and gave it a shake. "Jess," he said. "Don't do it again. Okay? 'Cause some things are just . . ." He waved in the general direction of his room, as if that one gesture gathered up everything that was his—all the bits and pieces of himself—in one grand sweep of his arm. "Some things are just private. You know?"

Jessie nodded her head. But she didn't have a clue what he was talking about.

Chapter 11
The Silence was a Bulldozer

metaphor (n) a figure of speech that says that one thing is another different thing as a way to compare the two and note their similarities; for example: "my mother is a battleship" or "school was a rollercoaster"

Mrs. Overton was sitting at her desk when the class filed in on Friday morning. Evan thought she looked really tired.

"How's Langston?" asked Christopher, dropping his completed love poem in the In basket on Mrs. Overton's desk.

"Better. He was very sick yesterday. We spent the

whole day at the animal hospital. He has pneumonia, which is serious for a cat as old as Langston. But the vet gave him some medicine and said he's going to be fine."

A bunch of kids were gathered around Mrs. Overton's desk to hear the latest on Langston's health and to hand in their love poems. Evan noticed another group, mostly girls, huddled around Jessie's desk. They wanted to know if Jessie had finished tallying the results of the survey, but Jessie wasn't giving anything away. Not yet.

Slowly, Evan pulled a piece of paper out of his backpack. He wished the kids standing around the teacher's desk would go back to their seats. He watched as Adam casually dropped his poem into the basket, as if it were just another math assignment. Evan knew that Adam had written his poem about playing basketball and Paul had written about his family's sailboat. Malik had written a poem about a bug, which he had recited to everyone on the playground that morning:

I dug a bug from under the rug.
The bug said hi and looked me in the eye.
I hugged my bug.
Bad idea!
Bye-bye bug.

Evan didn't think it really counted as a love poem, but it was pretty funny. He ambled over to Mrs. Overton's desk, his poem held low against his thigh. He watched and waited for the right moment, then slipped his poem, face-down, into the basket just before Nina and Ben put their poems on top of his.

All morning, he'd gone back and forth: Should he hand in the poem about his grandmother or the one about the tepee in the woods on his grandma's farm? His mom said both were good, but it was the one about Grandma that made his heart beat fast and his mouth go dry. At the last minute, he'd decided to play it safe and hand in the one about the tepee.

Several of the kids were telling Mrs. Overton about the second mysterious appearance of the candy hearts when Salley interrupted. "Tell us the truth, Mrs. O. Are you the one who left the candy hearts?"

"I am not," said Mrs. Overton solemnly.

"Yeah, but that's what you'd say if you *did* leave the hearts," said Ryan, and several kids agreed.

"That may be true, but I didn't leave them. And I'm glad there weren't any waiting on your desks this morning."

Evan was glad, too. He did not want to get another box of hearts with the kind of message you could find at Wal-Mart. He decided that if any more mysterious candy hearts appeared, he would throw his box in the trash without even looking at it.

"Morning Meeting, everyone," said Mrs. Overton, corralling them all to the rug. "Today, I have two poems in honor of my poor sick cat, who is now on the mend."

"Two poems!" shouted Jessie. "Give me a break!"

"I bet you're going to read us another poem by Langston Hughes," said David.

"No, but I think you'll see why I chose this poem, instead," said Mrs. Overton. "It's called 'Fog.'" She turned the easel paper with a giant flourish of her arm, as if she were unveiling a statue in the center of town. Salley read the poem out loud, and Evan followed the words silently.

FOG
by Carl Sandburg

The fog comes
on little cat feet.

It sits looking
over harbor and city
on silent haunches
and then moves on.

"It's a metaphor!" shouted Nina, pointing to the photo of Langston that said METAPHORS BE WITH YOU. Mrs. Overton had taught them how poets sometimes use one thing to mean something else.

"Yes!" said Mrs. Overton. "What's the metaphor?" Almost half the class raised their hands.

"The fog is a cat," answered Taffy.

"That's just what fog is like," said Maddy. "It's like a cat, the way it creeps around." And Evan agreed. He had never thought about it before, but now he would always think of a cat when he saw fog creeping across his backyard.

Jessie shook her head. "Fog is not like a cat. Not at all. Fog is vapor. It's drops of water in the air. A cat is an animal. It's a solid, and it's alive. The two are nothing alike."

What Jessie said was true, and yet—Evan could *see* it. He could see the fog with its long tail curling around the corner of a house, arching its back as it rubbed up against a building and purred. He could imagine fog purring. How did the poet do that?

"What about the second poem?" asked Megan.

Everyone looked expectantly at Mrs. Overton, and Evan thought he saw her face turn just the slightest bit pink.

"Well, the second poem is written by me, actually. I wrote it yesterday at the animal hospital."

116

"You wrote a poem?" asked Adam. "But you're a teacher!"

"Teachers can write poems," said Mrs. Overton. "Anyone can. I'm not saying mine is as good as Mr. Sandburg's, but it's mine, and I like it."

Evan couldn't believe that Mrs. Overton had written a poem. He leaned forward and watched as she turned the easel paper and began reading.

COUNTING RIBS

your head
too weak to lift I
lay my own alongside
yours and run my hand
across the silky familiar side of you
fingers feeling bone beneath
one   two   three

                              breathe
four   five   six

                              please
seven   eight   nine

                              breathe

counting to keep my
eyes from crying my
heart from breaking
out
of its own ribbed cage

breathe   please   breathe

On the last word, Mrs. Overton's voice cracked, and Evan—who had been staring intently at the words on the page—turned quickly to look at his teacher's face. Her eyes were swimming with tears, and her lip trembled just the slightest bit. Horrified, Evan looked around the room. Everyone was staring at Mrs. Overton. No one knew what to do. Teachers were not supposed to cry.

Megan was the first to respond. She jumped up from her spot on the rug and circled her arms around one of Mrs. Overton's arms. Then Maddy, Rachel, and Tessa clustered around her, too, laying their hands on her shoulders and arms, as if they were a protective fence that had sprung up out of nowhere. Most of the boys, including Evan, looked at their feet or the floor. The silence was a bulldozer, plowing them under.

Until Jessie spoke up.

"Why are you crying, Mrs. Overton?" she asked in a loud voice.

Mrs. Overton looked right at Jessie, but her voice was high-pitched and broken. "Because he was so sick, and I was afraid I was going to have to let him go. I've had him practically my whole life." Megan patted Mrs. Overton on the shoulder, and Evan could see that she was starting to cry, too.

"But that was yesterday," said Jessie. "You were sad *yesterday*. You said he's fine now. Aren't you happy now?"

"Yes, Jessie. He's going to be fine. But I guess the poem just carried me back to that feeling. That terrible, hopeless feeling when I thought I might lose him. That's what poems do. Take a feeling and make it real, right in the moment."

No one said anything as they thought about

what Mrs. Overton had just said. Then Evan spoke up in a clear voice. "It's a love poem," he said.

Mrs. Overton nodded her head. "Yes, it very much is." Her eyes filled up again, and she looked like she was really going to start crying now, right there in front of the whole class. It was just awful.

"And it's a good one," said Evan, pointing at the easel, "because of all those long *e* sounds. They sound like breathing, those long *e*'s. Like when you're sick and wheezing." He made a breathing-in-and-out sound that sounded like the vowel *e*.

"And it's got alliteration," said Salley. "See? 'Fingers' and 'feeling' and 'bone' and 'beneath.' That makes it good, too."

So then the class went through the poem and found all the examples of alliteration and assonance and rhyme, and the girls all sat down again, and Mrs. Overton's face went back to what a teacher's face is supposed to look like when she's teaching her fourth-graders about poetry.

After talking about the poem, Evan was quick to

get back to his seat, but it was Carly Brownell who reached inside her desk first and found something unexpected.

"Hey!" she shouted, raising her hand above her head and rattling the small box she held. "More candy hearts!"

Chapter 12
Breaking News

breaking news (n) a news story that is unfolding at the moment that reporters are reporting it

There was a mad scramble as all the kids in 4-O ran to their desks to look for boxes of candy hearts. Jessie's desk was very neat, so it took her no time to find hers. But other kids had to pull out crumpled papers and notebooks and pencil cases before they uncovered the familiar pink and red box with the little cellophane window. Everyone started rattling the boxes, and soon the room sounded like a maraca band in full swing.

"Mine says CAPTAIN JACK," shouted Jack Bagdasarian, and he growled like a pirate to show that he deserved the name.

"Look at mine!" said Michael Mahoney. "FLY HIGH!" Michael's dad was a commercial pilot, and Michael took lots of trips on airplanes.

Jessie carefully removed one of the hearts from her box and read the message. GOOD IDEAS. Where had she heard that before? She tried to think, but Mrs. Overton shouted out in a near panic, "Do not eat any of this candy!" and Jessie's attention switched to her teacher. Mrs. Overton looked like the cartoon character Wile E. Coyote when he realizes he's about to drop one thousand feet into a canyon. Jessie pulled out her reporter's notebook. This was breaking news, and she didn't want to miss anything.

"Where is this candy coming from?" asked Mrs. Overton.

"Can I please go to the bathroom?" asked Evan in a loud voice.

"Not right this second, Evan," said Mrs. Overton, rubbing a hand across her forehead.

"I need to go now!" Evan nearly shouted. Jessie

stared at her brother. Was he about to pee in his pants? But his face didn't have *that* kind of look on it. Instead, he looked like he was ready to rip someone's head off. What could Evan be mad about?

"Yes, go. But come straight back. We've got to figure out ..." Mrs. Overton didn't even seem to know how to finish her sentence.

Jessie watched as Evan grabbed the big wooden bathroom pass from the hook by the door, then stormed out of the room. There was something red in his hand. She made a note of this in her notebook.

> 8:42 am – Evan to
> Bathroom – Something
> red in his hand

A lot of the kids were circulating around the classroom, comparing candy-heart messages. Mrs. Overton stood with her hands on her hips for a moment, then made a beeline for the classroom phone. Meanwhile, Jessie meandered over to Evan's desk and took a quick peek inside. As expected, it was an atrocious mess, but there was no box of candy hearts.

8:44 am – Evan's desk – no hearts...

Jessie stooped down and looked under Evan's desk. "Jessie, you're not eating candy, are you?" asked Mrs. Overton, still talking on the phone.

"No, Mrs. O. I'm just looking for trash." If something was on the floor, it was trash. Everybody knew that.

"Nobody eat anything. Take your seats. I'm going to collect the candy—"

There was a shout from the classroom. "No way!" called out Scott. "I'm not giving mine up!" Almost everyone in the class was against the idea of Mrs. Overton confiscating their Valentine treat.

"Jessie, it's private property, right?" asked Tessa.

"Can a teacher take something that belongs to us? I mean, legally?"

At the beginning of the school year, Jessie had organized the entire class into a courtroom to put Scott Spencer on trial for the theft of two hundred and eight dollars. Whenever there was a question about the law, the kids in 4-O turned to Jessie.

Jessie shrugged. "We're kids." She'd learned the hard way that the legal system couldn't be counted on to fix the injustices of the world. "We're not even allowed to *own* property."

"Is that true, Mrs. Overton?" asked Paul.

"That stinks!" said Jack.

"You can take stuff from us?" said Ray. "That's not fair!"

"Look," said Mrs. Overton. "I just don't want anyone getting sick. We don't know where this candy is coming from."

"Nobody's gotten sick yet, and we've been eating these hearts all week," said David. "I'm pretty sure if they were poisoned, someone would have died by now."

The class agreed. When Mrs. Overton finally got

everyone to quiet down, Megan raised her hand. "Maybe you could let us take them home and let our parents decide?"

Evan walked back in the room at that moment, but no one noticed except Jessie. She watched him hang the bathroom pass on its hook, then return to his seat. He still had that angry look on his face, but it wasn't quite as bad as when he'd left the room. And his hands were empty. Jessie wrote this fact in her notebook.

8:49 am - Evan back
from bathroom -
HANDS EMPTY

"Listen up!" said Mrs. Overton, taking charge again. "I'm going to collect the candy hearts and keep them until I've had a chance to talk with Mrs. Fletcher. If she gives the go-ahead to send them home, it's okay with me. She's in charge of the school, so whatever she says goes." Mrs. Overton scooped up the paper collection basket on her desk. "Everyone grab your candy hearts and line up for music. I'm going to collect your boxes as you file out."

Jessie was glad she wasn't line leader for the week. She hung at the back of the line, determined to be last. When she got in place, David, who was in the middle of the line, ducked out and came to the back to stand behind her.

"Why did you do that?" asked Jessie, annoyed. The line began to move forward.

"Do what?" asked David.

"Leave the line and go to the end."

"I didn't cut."

"I didn't say you did. I asked why you left the line." Jessie noticed that Evan was saying something to Mrs. Overton and that Mrs. Overton did not look happy.

David shrugged. "I wasn't really in line."

"Yes, you were," said Jessie, shaking her head and thinking that David Kirkorian was sometimes the most annoying kid in class.

"I'm allowed to stand where I want to. It's a free country." David folded his arms across his chest and stared straight over Jessie's head. He was about a foot taller than her, so he could do that without even trying.

When they reached the door, Jessie dropped her box of candy hearts into the basket. She didn't mind giving it up. Candy hearts had never been her favorite. She didn't like the way they scraped against her teeth.

Jessie waited until they were halfway down the hall before she said to Mrs. Overton, "I need to go back to the classroom for a second." Mrs. Overton was carrying the basket full of candy, and Jessie knew she was taking it to the office to consult with Mrs. Fletcher while the class was in music. There was no way Mrs. Overton was going to escort her back to the classroom. She was too distracted by the mystery of the candy hearts.

"Can it wait?" asked Mrs. Overton.

"No, it's something I really need. I'll be one second."

"Be quick. And then straight to music!" Mrs. Overton veered left and disappeared into the office as the line of students headed to the music room.

Jessie scooted past David, hurrying back to the classroom.

"I'll come with you," said David.

Jessie whirled around. "You will not!" The *last* thing she wanted was David Kirkorian witnessing what she was about to do. David practically jumped back and then stood there, with a look on his face that Jessie couldn't figure out—even if she'd had a million years to study it.

She ran down the hall, but before she got to her classroom, she stopped in front of the boys' bathroom. She wished her friend Maxwell were here. Not only was Maxwell a terrific spy, but he was also a boy. Which would have made this next part of her mission easier.

Still, if you're going to be an investigative reporter, you have to be willing to do the dirty work of investigating. As her grandmother said, it was time to break some eggs.

Jessie pushed open the door of the boys' bathroom and called out, "Anyone in here?" No one answered.

This bathroom was different from hers! What were those strange white sink things on the wall? Jessie stared and stared but couldn't figure them out.

Suddenly, she heard a noise in the hall and remembered how much trouble she would be in if someone found her in the boys' bathroom. She hurried to the trash can, pushed open the flap door, and peeked inside.

There it was.

Evan's box of candy hearts. She tried to reach in to pluck it out, but her arm was nowhere near long enough. She tugged on the top of the trash can and after a minute, the top came off. It was heavier than she thought it would be, and when she put it down on the hard tile floor, it made a loud clanking noise that made her heart jump.

Jessie wasn't a lot taller than the trash can, so wrestling it over and laying it on its side wasn't easy.

But she finally managed it, and this time she was careful not to let the metal trash can clang to the floor. She got down on her knees and peered inside, but the trash had resettled and now the candy box was nowhere in sight.

Without warning, the door to the bathroom swung open and two small boys walked in. They were so little that Jessie figured they must be A.M. kindergarteners. They had their arms around each other's shoulders, and they were singing a song.

But they stopped as soon as they saw Jessie.

"You're not supposed to be in here!" said one of the boys.

"Neither are you," said Jessie. It was a dumb thing to say, but it was all she could think of on the spot.

"Why not?" asked the other boy. The first boy's hand crept up to his face, and he started to suck his thumb.

"Because . . . you have to go. Now!" The last word came out loud, like a fire alarm. Both boys jumped and then ran for the door.

Jessie knew she had about thirty seconds before a custodian or teacher came running into the bathroom to investigate. She began to pluck out wet and crumpled paper towels. Touching all those dirty, used, boy paper towels made her stomach heave, but she did it anyway.

There it was! She grabbed the cardboard box and ran out of the bathroom, looking behind her to see whether someone was coming after her. But nobody seemed to notice her at all.

When she got to her own cubby, she stopped and pretended to straighten her jacket as she examined the box she'd plucked from the trash can. The cardboard was smashed as if it had been stomped on by a herd of elephants, and the candy hearts inside were nothing more than crushed powder. But she found one piece of a heart that still had a few letters on it.

Chapter 13
As Heavy as a Wet Blanket

simile (n) a comparison of one thing with another using "like" or "as"

Evan woke up on Saturday morning in a bad mood. It was the same mood he'd gone to bed with on Friday night. The same mood that had followed him all that day, hanging over his shoulders like a heavy, wet, stinky wool blanket.

But after he'd complained to his mother for ten solid minutes about the lack of milk in the house and then snapped at Jessie for leaving her shoes on the stairs right where he would trip over them, both his mother and Jessie declared that he was a beast and told him to get out of the house until he turned back into a human being.

He decided to grab his snowshoes and hike through the woods and into the cemetery. There were good trees for climbing there, and it was his favorite place to think. He went to the garage and started rummaging through the big plastic bin of outdoor stuff. About four inches of snow had fallen last night, and although he could have gone out in just his boots, it was more fun to wear snowshoes.

He started hunting through the shelves in the garage. Instead of finding his own snowshoes, though, he found his dad's. They were behind the pile of sleds, Boogie Boards, and Skim Disks, wedged between the wall and the shelving unit.

Evan scowled. Things that used to belong to his dad were always turning up. He'd be looking on the bookshelf for one of his old Calvin and Hobbes books, and he'd find a book on fly-fishing instead. Or he'd be reaching all the way to the back of the linen closet for a clean pillowcase, and there would be his dad's old Michigan Wolverines hat. Evan hated finding these reminders. He figured, what's done is done. There was no point in even thinking about the past.

But this time, he looked at the snowshoes and then at his own feet. He'd been growing a lot this year. He was the second tallest boy in his class. Maybe his dad's old snowshoes would fit him.

He sat down and adjusted the toe straps to their smallest setting. Then he jammed the toes of his boots into the straps and cinched the heel straps as tight as they would go. He stood up and took a few scratchy steps across the concrete garage floor. The snowshoes stayed on.

Out in the cemetery, the snow had drifted and banked so that some spots were several feet deep, but others were covered by no more than a dusting. Evan decided to circle the whole cemetery once, then do a double crisscross through the middle and end up at the Civil War monument, which was made from three old cannons welded together. That way he'd be hot and sweaty, and sitting on the cold metal would feel good.

When he finally dropped his snowshoes and started to haul himself to the top of the monument, he was glad he'd put on gloves. The cannons were freezing cold, and getting to the top was like shimmying up a giant black icicle. But Evan was good at climbing, and he made it to the top without too much slipping and sliding.

Once he was there, though, that feeling of power that usually came over him—the one that made him want to shout "I am the king of the world!"—didn't come. Instead, it was as if the heavy, wet blanket had followed him, and now it draped itself over his shoulders, just as before. What was the point of getting out of the house if you couldn't ditch your bad mood?

And then something even worse happened. Walking up the back path from the opposite end of the cemetery with her old, half-blind dog came Megan Moriarty. She was the last person Evan wanted to see—or be seen with—and he quickly looked around to check for anyone who might be watching them. But the cemetery was empty.

Megan was nearly at the monument before she noticed Evan. She had her head down because of the wind, and her dog trailed behind her as if he was having trouble keeping up. When she caught sight of him, Megan stood up tall and waved enthusiastically, a big smile lighting up her face.

Evan barely nodded, then looked the other way. He couldn't pretend he hadn't seen her, but he sure as heck wasn't going to give her the idea that he cared she was there.

"What are you doing up there?" Megan asked as she walked up to the base of the monument.

"Nothing," said Evan, and shrugged to show that she wasn't going to get any more out of him.

"I'll come up." Megan turned to her dog and said, "Sit. Stay." Then she put one foot on the lowest cannon.

"There isn't room. And it's slippery. You'd probably get hurt."

Megan stopped, took her foot down, then stared

up at him. Evan was careful to look off in the distance, as if he'd forgotten that she was even there. The wind had picked up again, and it was really cold on top of the monument. Evan half wished he could climb down. For a split second he imagined the two of them heading back to his house for hot chocolate, but he pushed *that* thought out of his head. Instead, he let the beastliness rise up in him again, and he said, "Dogs aren't allowed in the cemetery. It's a new rule."

"Nobody ever told me that," said Megan. "We always walk him here."

"Well, you've just been lucky, that's all. If the police see you walking your dog, they'll fine you twenty-five dollars." He didn't really know what the fine was, and he'd never seen the police stop anyone for walking a dog in the cemetery. But there *was* a sign by the caretaker's house.

Megan seemed unsure about what to do. She picked up the dog's leash, but then just stood there, looking around her. Maybe she was checking for the police. She wasn't smiling anymore.

"I guess . . . do you want to go sledding later? You and Jessie? My mom will take us over to the high school."

Evan shook his head and continued to look off in the distance. "Nah. I've got things to do. Maybe Jessie will go with you."

"Okay. Well . . . I guess . . . I'll see you on Monday?" Then she laughed. "Valentine's Day!"

Evan scowled. "What a stupid holiday. I wish they'd never invented it."

"What's so bad about Valentine's Day?" asked Megan, giving her dog a scratch behind the ears. "You get candy."

"Yeah, like those crummy candy hearts. No one even wants those things. And those stupid messages!"

Megan stood up straight. "What's wrong with the messages? Everyone likes them."

Evan was about to say "I didn't," but there was no way he was going to tell her that he was the only one who didn't get a personal message.

Besides, he didn't want anyone to see him talking to Megan Moriarty as if they *liked* each other.

"Whatever. Hey, I gotta go." He slid down the cannon, and when he landed he grabbed his snowshoes and kept going, bounding down the hill without even looking back. The sooner Megan figured out that he didn't want to talk to her, the better. Anything else was just too complicated.

Chapter 14
Tip

tip (n) information passed to a reporter

"Maxwell, I've got a problem," Jessie said. She was lying on her bed, with the phone pressed close to her ear.

There was no response from the other end of the line. Jessie knew Maxwell was there, because she could hear him breathing.

"Why aren't you saying anything?" Jessie asked.

"You didn't ask me a question," said Maxwell in his usual flat voice.

"So? When someone says 'I've got a problem,' you're supposed to say something like 'Really?' or 'What is it?' or 'Tell me about it.'" Jessie sometimes found it exasperating that she had to explain these simple things to Maxwell. But that's just the way Maxwell was. She waited a minute to see what he would say, but then she just gave up. "Oh, for Pete's sake! Here's my problem."

She told Maxwell about the survey and the mysterious candy hearts and how no one knew who had drawn the heart on the door in the bathroom.

"I was going to write an article called 'The Candy Heart Mystery,' but I haven't solved that one yet. And I haven't figured out the secret on the bathroom wall, either!" Jessie had been reading an Encyclopedia Brown mystery before calling Maxwell. She loved the way each chapter contained clues to solve a mystery, and the way the answer to each mystery was revealed in the "Answers" section at the back of the book. If she knew the answers to the two mysteries in 4-O, *then* she'd have a blockbuster front-page story. "I don't know," she continued. "Maybe I should just use the survey as my front-page story. Everyone seems pretty interested in that. Which story do *you* think I should put on the front page?"

"I don't know."

"I know you don't *know*. I'm asking for your opinion."

"I don't have an opinion."

Jessie tugged on a thread that was hanging off her jeans. "If I only *knew* who was sending the candy hearts. Or who wrote the heart on the bathroom door."

"Maybe it's the same person," said Maxwell.

"That would be the story of the century!" Jessie's head practically exploded thinking about what a success her newspaper would be if she revealed the answer to both mysteries. Kids would be fighting over *The 4-O Forum*. Maybe she'd even get an award, like the Pulitzer Prize.

"I bet I could figure out who wrote the heart on the bathroom door," said Maxwell. Maxwell had a gift for seeing details and patterns that other people missed, but Jessie was sure that even Maxwell couldn't match the handwriting with anyone else's in the class.

"No, I tried," she said. "I've been looking at

everyone's writing, and no one makes their *M*s and *E*s and *T*s like that."

"Then match the heart," said Maxwell.

"What do you mean?"

"Figure out who draws a heart that looks like the one in the bathroom and you'll catch the thief."

"We're not looking for a thief!" said Jessie. "It's just someone who wrote something dumb on a bathroom wall. Probably a fifth-grader!"

"Follow the heart," Maxwell said in a voice that sounded deep and spooky. "Follow the heart."

Jessie sat quietly for a minute thinking to herself. This was an idea that hadn't occurred to her, and she thought it was the best tip she'd received all week. Then she said, "Maxwell, you are a genius."

"Yep," said Maxwell. Jessie could hear the quiet music of his favorite computer game starting up on his end of the line. "I'm Maxwell. And I'm smart."

After she got off the phone with Maxwell, Jessie wandered down to the basement and started digging through some stuff that was piled in one corner. She had to push her way past a box of kindling, a folding card table, and a big cardboard cutout of Darth Vader, but she finally got to what she was looking for: the signs from last summer during the Lemonade War. One of them she stared at long and hard. It had a picture of a cat sipping a tall glass of lemonade—and sprinkled in the corner were a few cutout paper hearts. She hadn't made *those* hearts.

Then she walked over to the craft table and rummaged through the messy pile of scrap paper. When she found a certain sheet of pink construction paper, she held it up and stared at the leftover hole.

"Aha," said Jessie in a whisper.

Chapter 15
Valentine's Night

consonance (n) the repetition of the same sounds (particularly consonants) within words that are nearby

It was when the shadows grew long and the last streak of winter sunlight sank behind the trees that Grandma was at her worst. There was something about the dying light that brought on her confusion, as if the shadows and dark corners of the house held her memories, and she couldn't quite see them anymore. They were there, but just out of reach.

Evan walked into the kitchen a little after five o'clock and found Grandma in front of the open pantry. She was pulling cans and boxes off the shelves, stacking them up on the floor all around her. Usually she napped until six, waking up just in time for dinner, but sometimes she had trouble settling down. Evan noticed that her shirt was untucked and her feet were bare. Not a good sign.

"Hey, Grandma," said Evan. He had learned not to come too close to Grandma when she was confused without first giving her a little warning. Sometimes, it made her feel scared when Evan walked up to her too quickly.

"This is bad," said Grandma. "We don't have any of the things we need."

Evan wondered whether he should go upstairs and get his mother, then remembered that she had gone to the hardware store. She would be back soon. He had to keep his grandmother calm until his mother came back. "What do we need?" he asked.

"Well, everything. It's going to be a very long winter. And we don't have . . . anything." She swept her hand in front of the pantry, which was overflowing with food. "There are no beans. No tomatoes. Squash. Corn. Peppers. Applesauce. Nothing! We're going to starve this winter! You can't live on love, you know!"

Evan slowly inched his way across the room. His grandmother had grown up on a farm where they had raised most of the food they ate. And even though her farm wasn't really a "working" farm anymore, she still kept an enormous vegetable garden there through the summer and canned every fall. Evan always loved to look at the rows and rows of sealed glass jars cooling on the shelves in the canning shed when Grandma put up peaches and plums from the trees on her farm.

But what would become of the garden this summer now that Grandma lived with them? Evan imagined the tangled overgrowth, the choking weeds, the fence fallen down.

"We've got some tomatoes," said Evan. "See?" He opened another cupboard and pulled down a store-bought can of tomatoes.

Grandma walked quickly across the room and snatched up the can. She could move surprisingly fast for an eighty-year-old woman. "What is this?

What *is* this?" She put the can on the floor and immediately started rummaging through the newly opened cupboard. *Uh-oh,* thought Evan. *That was a mistake.* He had to think of something to calm her down, something to distract her from the food in the cupboards, or else the entire floor would be covered in food and it would take hours to put everything away.

"Grandma, did you know today is Valentine's Day?" It was actually the day before Valentine's Day, but Evan was betting his grandmother wouldn't know that.

"It isn't day at all," said Grandma, waving absently at the window.

"Well, Valentine's Night, then. Okay?"

"Hmmph," said Grandma, not slowing down a bit. She had gotten into the baking stuff and was hauling out bags of flour and cornmeal. "We can use this," she said, setting aside the five-pound bag of sugar.

"I have a valentine for you. Do you want to see it?" Evan was starting to feel a little desperate. When

Grandma got like this, there was no telling what direction she might go in. He looked at the clock: five fifteen. When would his mother get back from her errand?

"Come on," he said, gently taking her hand and pulling her away from the cupboard. "I'll show you your valentine." Luckily, she came along without a fight. His grandmother might be old, but she was still strong, and Evan was glad he didn't have to tussle with her.

Halfway up the stairs, she asked, "Where are we going?"

Evan said, "I have a valentine for you. Today is Valentine's Day."

His grandmother smiled. "I love Valentine's Day." Then a few steps later she asked, "Where are we going?"

In his room, Evan gently seated his grandmother on the edge of his bed. He was glad Jessie's door was closed and had the Locked sign up. She had been working all day on her newspaper, and Evan hoped she'd stay in there until their mother got home. Jessie didn't like seeing Grandma confused. It made her anxious, and then she'd start to shout, which made the situation worse. Evan would have to handle this alone.

"See?" he said. "I wrapped it and everything." He handed the package to his grandmother, wondering if she would open it. You could never be sure with Grandma these days.

"For me?" She giggled. "I love surprises. Thank you!" Quickly she tore off the paper, then read aloud the framed poem that Evan had copied over five times until he got it just right.

> a tree(doesn't have)
> knees that creak
>> but
>> Grandma
>> does
> a tree(wouldn't forget)
> my name
>> but
>> Grandma
>> did

a tree(stands tall)
and proud
and good
  and
  Grandma
  is

  a tree

She looked at it, then smiled at him, clearly not understanding. "For me?" she asked.

Evan nodded. "I wrote that poem for you." He didn't mind showing his poem to Grandma. His secret love of poetry was safe with her.

"It's very nice. You did a good job." She placed her hand on top of his and patted it several times. "You're a good boy," she said, and Evan could tell that she didn't quite know who he was just then, that the memory of him was beyond her reach, hiding in one of the dark corners of her mind. "I have . . . I'd like to give you something, too. I have a poem for you." She stood up, as tall and straight as a pine tree, and recited,

i carry your heart with me(i carry it in
my heart)i am never without it(anywhere
i go you go,my dear;and whatever is done
by only me is your doing,my darling)
                                        i fear
no fate(for you are my fate,my sweet)i want
no world(for beautiful you are my world,my true)
and it's you are whatever a moon has always meant
and whatever a sun will always sing is you

here is the deepest secret nobody knows
(here is the root of the root and the bud of the bud
and the sky of the sky of a tree called life;which grows
higher than soul can hope or mind can hide)
and this is the wonder that's keeping the stars apart

i carry your heart(i carry it in my heart)

Evan's grandmother sat down and picked up his
hand and patted it again. She was smiling and her
eyes were shining. "That's a poem by E. E. Cummings. He's my favorite poet of all time."
Evan stared at his grandmother as if he'd never

seen her before. "I didn't know you knew poetry, Grandma!"

"Oh, yes. It's a requirement. We have to memorize and recite a poem every year. I'm quite good at it. The best in my class." She looked down at the framed poem in her hand. "This is a very nice poem. Did E. E. Cummings write it?"

Evan bent his head toward his grandmother.

"Yes. He wrote it just for you."

Chapter 16
Front-Page Layout

front-page layout (n) the way in which text and pictures are arranged on the front page of a newspaper so that all the space is used and the headlines catch the reader's attention

Jessie knew in her heart that today was going to be a great day. She closed her closet door and picked up her backpack from beside her bed. Then she grabbed the grocery bag that held twenty-eight copies of *The 4-O Forum*. She had gotten up early this morning to finish printing and folding them. They were ready to go!

She reached in the bag and pulled out one of the

copies of the paper. She held it up so she could admire the front page. It was perfect! The headline was a grabber, the columns of type were neat and straight, and the whole page was filled, which was really important because there should never be empty space in a real newspaper.

That had been tricky. Yesterday, when she'd finished laying out the front-page article, including all her terrific pie charts, she'd still had a box of empty space to fill. It wasn't all that big, just about three inches in the last column, but Jessie knew she couldn't leave it empty. What could she fill it with?

Then she'd had a brilliant idea. She would put Evan's poem in that space. It fit perfectly! And she could just imagine how thrilled he would be to have his writing published in a newspaper. For everyone to see. He would probably shout with excitement. She decided to make it a surprise.

Then she turned the paper over and looked at the back page. She had written the double article about the candy heart mystery *and* the secret on the bathroom wall just like a chapter from an Encyclopedia Brown book. The reader could solve the mystery because all the clues were sprinkled throughout the newspaper in pictures and articles. But you had to go to the back page of the newspaper to find the answer. Jessie couldn't help smiling when she saw the answer printed in a framed rectangle on the back page. It was a masterpiece!

"Jessie, did you strip your bed like I asked?" called Mrs. Treski from downstairs. Monday was laundry day in the Treski household, and each child was responsible for taking the sheets off the bed and bringing them down to the laundry room.

"I don't have time!" shouted Jessie, not wanting to wait even one more minute to get to school with her blockbuster newspaper.

"You have plenty of time. Do it now, Missy Miss!"

There was no point in arguing with her mother. Especially about laundry. She put down the grocery bag and dropped her backpack to the floor. Then she pulled the bed away from the wall so she could take off the blanket and sheets.

Something fell to the floor.

Jessie peered down into the space between the bed and the wall. There was a folded-up piece of paper on the floor. With a sinking heart, Jessie reached down and picked it up.

It was the twenty-seventh survey, the one she hadn't been able to find on Thursday! Jessie sat down hard on the bed. The image of Langston shouting NUMERATOR ON TOP, DENOMINATOR ON BOTTOM! jumped into her mind. She had used a denominator of twenty-six for all her calculations, but now the correct number was twenty-seven! That meant that every statistic in her front-page story was wrong. The whole article was a mistake! And there wasn't time to fix it before school.

Everything was ruined.

Who did this? she wanted to scream, shaking the piece of paper as if it were somehow at fault. She knew that no one was to blame, but still she wanted to be angry at *someone.* Quickly she looked at the survey to see if she could tell whose it was.

Jessie stared and stared at the creased paper. She didn't recognize the handwriting, but that wasn't surprising.

Who could it be?

She looked at the paper again. It was strange. Someone in 4-O *like*-liked her. What did that mean? How was she supposed to feel? It was a puzzle. But not the kind she could figure out.

Jessie folded the paper in half and put it in her backpack. At recess she would have to recalculate the results of the survey. That was the important thing: making her newspaper a success. And it couldn't be a success if it didn't have the right numbers in it. She would think about someone liking her another time.

When the morning bell rang, Jessie hurried straight to her cubby and put the newspapers at the very bottom, where her boots usually went. Then she covered up the bag with her coat and put her boots on top of that. She didn't want anybody getting at those papers until she had a chance to correct them.

But when she turned to go into the classroom, she suddenly realized that in all the activity of the morning—the laundry, her excitement about the newspaper, the surprise discovery of the missing survey, not to mention the shock of finding out that someone in the class had a crush on her!—she had forgotten to go to the bathroom before leaving the house. Oh, great! This day was just getting better and better!

She hurried to the girls' bathroom in her hallway, peeked in to make sure the bathroom was empty, then headed for the second-to-last stall.

She was about to push open the door when she noticed two shoes on the other side of it. And she recognized those shoes!

"What are you doing in here?" asked Jessie. She really did have to go to the bathroom. This was no time to chat.

Megan didn't answer. Instead, Jessie heard a strange noise that sounded like someone gargling.

"Are you okay?" Jessie waited. "Why aren't you talking?"

A sound came out of the bathroom stall that even Jessie recognized.

"Why are you crying?" Jessie couldn't figure this out. Why would someone cry in a bathroom, of all places? "Do you need the nurse?"

"No!" said Megan.

"Well, I have to go to the bathroom."

"So go to the bathroom!"

"I only use this one. You have to come out."

"No!"

"Then . . ." Jessie didn't know what she could do, but whatever it was, it was going to have to be *soon*. She shifted her weight from one foot to the other and then back again.

Suddenly the door opened and Megan stepped out. Her eyes were red from crying, and there were tears on her cheeks. She looked terrible. In her hands, she had a wad of wet paper towels. "Go ahead!" she said, rushing past Jessie as if she didn't want to be seen.

"Well, wait for me to finish," said Jessie, who hurried in before disaster struck. When she came back out, Megan was standing at the sink. Jessie washed her hands carefully, singing the ABC song under her breath to make sure she got rid of all the germs on her hands. Then she pointed at the door of the bathroom stall and asked Megan, "How come you were trying to wipe off the heart you drew?"

"Who says *I* drew it?" asked Megan, sounding angry.

"Because the heart in the stall looks like the hearts you drew on our lemonade stand. All weird and off center. And then you cut one like that out of paper at my house." Jessie pointed at the empty bathroom stall. "You disguised your handwriting, but you forgot to disguise the heart."

Megan's face crumpled and she started to cry again.

"Oh, for Pete's sake," said Jessie. "Here!" She pulled three dry paper towels out of the dispenser and handed them to Megan. "Look, do this." Jessie took back one of the paper towels and bunched it up, crumpling and uncrumpling it five or six times. "It makes it softer. See?"

Megan took the paper towel from Jessie and wiped her eyes, then took a few deep breaths. "Can you still see it?" she asked, looking at the bathroom door.

"Uh-huh. It's lighter, but you can still read it," said Jessie. She bent down to retie her shoe, then stood up. "I don't get it. *You* drew the heart. How come you're trying to wipe it off?"

"Because now, it's just—embarrassing!"

"Then why did you draw it in the first place?" shouted Jessie. This kind of conversation didn't make sense. Megan drew the heart, then she got mad at Jessie for asking about it! And writing on a bathroom wall! It was crazy the way she was acting.

Megan nodded her head. "I couldn't resist. It's like I *had* to write it on the wall. I couldn't stop myself."

Jessie shook her head. "You need to exercise better impulse control." That's what her mother said to her sometimes.

"What can I say?" said Megan sadly. "This is what happens when you're in love." She heaved a deep, shuddery sigh and stared at the crumpled paper towels in her hand. "You know what I mean?"

Jessie stared at her. "I have no idea what you're talking about."

"Well, lucky you," said Megan glumly. She wiped her nose with one of the paper towels. "Hey, Jess? Why doesn't Evan like me? I thought we were friends."

"What do you mean 'like'?" Jessie thought of the survey results, and one paper in particular—a paper whose handwriting she *did* know, almost as well as her own.

"You know what I mean. Do you think he *likes* me?"

Jessie stiffened up. "I'm not authorized to talk about it. I took an oath of secrecy." She thought of question number four on the survey. "Besides 37 percent of the class thinks you should tell him yourself." Oh, brother. Even that statistic was wrong now. Jessie really had her work cut out for her.

"Seriously?"

"Well, approximately. If everyone stopped treating this love stuff like it was top secret, the whole thing would be a lot easier. It still wouldn't make any sense, but it would be easier."

"Maybe you're right," said Megan thoughtfully.

"We're going to be late," said Jessie. "I don't like being late."

"Yeah, okay. Friends?" Megan stuck her hand out, but Jessie knew that Megan hadn't washed her hands after she came out of the stall, so Jessie just patted Megan on the shoulder and said, "Absolutely."

Then they both hurried back to the classroom. It was Valentine's Day, and there was a lot to do.

Chapter 17
Despair Deeper Than the Ocean

hyperbole (n) an extremely exaggerated statement

"Evan, is Jessie absent today?" asked Mrs. Overton, holding her attendance book in her hands. Mrs. Overton had a pink heart pinned to her red sweater in honor of Valentine's Day. Near the end of the day, the kids would distribute their valentines to one another, placing the cards in the shoeboxes they'd decorated last week.

"Nope. She's here somewhere." The kids in 4-O had all settled down to their morning work, but a few desks were empty. Evan noticed that Jessie, Megan, Chaz, and Sarah were all missing. He was glad Megan was out. Evan didn't want to have to deal with his friends making jokes about Megan and him on Valentine's Day. Plus, he didn't want to see the hurt look on her face when he ignored her. All in all, it was good that she was absent. Even though there was a part of him that felt disappointed.

A few minutes later both Jessie and Megan walked into the classroom and took their seats.

"Girls, you're late," said Mrs. Overton, then stopped when she caught sight of Megan's face. "Don't let it happen again, okay?"

"Mrs. Overton?" said Jessie. "Can I stay in at recess and work on my newspaper? I need to fix a few things before I hand it out. It's a special Valentine's Day edition."

"Ooooh," said Scott Spencer, and some of the boys laughed. Evan stared at his morning work paper. He was not going to get involved in this conversation.

"Jessie, are you going to tell us about the survey?" asked Rachel.

"Yeah, we want to know about that. You promised," said Taffy.

Jessie smiled and faced the class. "Yes. The full—and accurate—results of the survey will be included on the front page of the newspaper. Along with some special features. First, a sweet mystery will be solved"—Jessie looked straight at Megan when she said this—"*and* there will be a poem by a surprise poet."

Evan watched as Jessie turned her gaze on him and flashed him a smile.

"What survey?" asked Mrs. Overton.

"A love survey!" shouted Scott Spencer. And the boys started making kissing noises and whooping it up.

"Jessie?"

"It's just a survey I handed out. All the kids answered it. Mrs. Feeney said it was okay!" Evan listened as Jessie's voice got squeaky in the way it did when she was nervous.

Mrs. Overton stared straight at Jessie, then tapped her pencil on her desktop. "I want to see your newspaper before you hand it out, okay? I'll look at it during recess. Meanwhile"—she turned her attention to the whole class—"I wanted to update you on the boxes of candy hearts that I collected from you on Friday."

"Confiscated!" shouted Scott Spencer, whose mother was a lawyer.

"Private property," called out David K.

"Power to the people!" yelled out Malik, then shrugged his shoulders to show he was just goofing around.

"Excuse me," said Mrs. Overton, lifting one eyebrow in the way she did when she was warning them to settle down. Evan always marveled at this technique. He'd never met anyone who could lift one eyebrow as high as Mrs. Overton. "As I was saying, I spoke with Mrs. Fletcher and she in turn spoke with the superintendent, and it has been decided that because we do not know the *source* of the candy, we cannot allow you to *have* the candy."

"Oh, come on!" shouted several of the kids in the class.

"It's just candy, for crying out loud!" said Ray.

"And it's Valentine's Day," said Salley.

"Yeah!" shouted most of the class in agreement.

"Enough! As I said, it has been decided." Mrs. Overton looked severely around the room.

Good, thought Evan. *No more stupid candy hearts.*

Jessie raised her hand. "Mrs. Overton, what if we did know where the candy came from? Would that make a difference?"

Mrs. Overton looked at her, perplexed. "Jessie, do you want to talk with me privately?"

"No." Jessie's face had that blank-slate look that left most people confused. But Evan knew that something was going on inside Jessie's head.

"Well," said Mrs. Overton. "I suppose it might make a difference if we knew who left the candy. Or maybe not. It would depend."

Just then a voice came over the PA announcing that an assembly for the lower grades had been canceled. When the announcement ended, Mrs. Overton told them to break into their rainforest groups. They were going to continue working on their group projects.

Evan looked around the room for his group and found them gathering at the back table. But his mind wasn't on the great kapok tree as he joined them. He was wondering why Jessie had looked straight at him when she mentioned the surprise poem in the newspaper? Was it a poem that Evan particularly liked?

And then an awful thought came to him. What if it was the framed poem he had given to Grandma? Jessie must have noticed it on Grandma's dresser and copied it to put in the paper. For everyone to see. Evan's head sank into his hands, and he groaned.

Chapter 18
Kill

kill (v) to *not* publish a story or newspaper that is ready (or close to ready) for publication

It didn't take a super detective to figure out that Mrs. Overton was not going to let Jessie hand out her newspaper to the class. Jessie didn't understand why, but there was something about this love stuff that made people act crazy. One look at Mrs. Overton's face when she'd heard "love survey" told Jessie that Mrs. Overton was going to put an end to this extra credit project before it even happened. She was going to kill the Valentine's Day issue of *The 4-O Forum,* and Jessie couldn't bear that thought. All her hard work—counting up the surveys, writing the articles, digging through the boys' trash—all for nothing. She would never have another front-page story like this one. A story that *everybody* would want to read. It was her one chance to be a star reporter, just like her dad. Even if her statistics were a little bit off, it was now or never.

"Well," said Jessie to the empty classroom. "I guess it's time to break some eggs." So while Mrs. Overton met with the principal to try to figure out what to do about the canceled assembly, Jessie walked out to the hallway and retrieved the bag of newspapers from her locker. Then she put on her hat, scarf, mittens, coat, and boots and headed out to the playground. *I'll be like one of those old-fashioned newsboys,* she thought, and imagined standing in the middle of the playground, shouting, "Extra! Extra! Read all about it!"

As she approached the picnic tables, Jessie surveyed the scene. Almost half the class was playing a sloppy game of soccer on the far end of the playground. There didn't seem to be real teams; it looked like everyone was running over the packed-down snow, chasing after the ball just to keep warm. About ten kids were swarming over the Green Machine, which was the large painted metal climbing structure in the middle of the playground. The last four or five kids were on the swings, hanging on to the cold metal chains as if their mittens were frozen on solid. Except for David Kirkorian. He was walking around the perimeter of the playground by himself, which is what he usually did during recess.

Jessie watched as Megan jumped off her swing and ran over to her.

"Jessie!" said Megan. "What did you mean when you said a mystery was going to be solved? What mystery?" Jessie looked at Megan's face and could tell that she was worried. Worry was an easy feeling to spot.

"The mystery of the candy hearts," said Jessie. "I know who sent them."

Megan stared back blankly, her mouth slightly open. After a minute, she asked, "Who?"

"You! I finally figured it out. All the clues were there. But first I had to figure out that *you* were the one who wrote the message in the bathroom. As soon as I figured that out, then I knew that you were the one who gave the candy hearts."

Megan shook her head. "How?"

"Easy. The Mystery Candy-Giver wrote *true* messages on everyone's hearts. Evan's hearts said I LOVE YOU. They had to be from you because you love Evan." Jessie crossed her arms, the mystery solved. "Plus, you wrote GOOD IDEAS on my hearts, and that's what you wrote on my comment card at the end of last summer. Remember?"

Jessie reached into her pocket and pulled out the comment card that she had saved so carefully for all these months.

> You're a really nice person and you have good ideas all the time. You're fun to be with and I'm glad you're my friend.

"And"—she raised her index finger like a wise philosopher—"your uncle owns a candy factory." Then Jessie smiled and held up a copy of the newspaper and showed Megan the front-page story.

"It's all in there?" asked Megan, looking miserable.

"Yep," said Jessie proudly. "Everyone's going to know—you're the one who gave them the candy! They're going to love you!"

"Jessie! Don't you see? Everyone's going to *know!*" Megan's face went wobbly, and Jessie noticed tears pooling in her eyes. Was Megan crying? Why would she cry?

But before she could ask, Evan came barreling over. "Jessie, I need to talk to you. Alone."

He grabbed Jessie's arm and started to pull her away, but stopped when Jessie said, "Megan's crying."

Evan turned to look at Megan. "Why is *she* crying?"

"Because she's the one who gave everyone the candy hearts and . . ." Jessie shrugged her shoulders.

There was just no way to make sense out of any of this love stuff.

"You?" said Evan, his voice rising in anger. "You're the one who wrote those messages?"

Megan nodded weakly.

Chapter 19
Megan Moriarty

alliteration (n) when the same letter or sound occurs at the beginning of words that are next to each other or nearby

Evan took a step back from Jessie and Megan and drove his hands into the pockets of his coat. "Well, that was just not nice. I mean, I don't *care,* but if you're going to write personal messages to everyone in the class, then you shouldn't leave one person out."

Megan shook her head in disgust. "I didn't, you dumb jerk."

"Yes, you did!" Evan was really angry now. His hearts were just store bought while everyone else's were made especially for them. He couldn't even show them to anyone! He'd had to hide them away or throw them in the trash. And it was *Megan* who had done such a mean thing? He had thought they were friends. He had liked her. *Like*-liked her.

Megan wasn't crying now. She looked like she was going to punch him in the nose. "Those messages *were* just for you. You were the only one who got them. They were the most special of all."

Evan stopped. What was she saying? He thought back to the three boxes of candy hearts he'd received. FOR YOU. BE MINE. I ♡ YOU.

Suddenly, Evan's stomach dropped down to his ankles. "Oh," was all he said. Then he crossed his arms and stared off at his friends playing soccer.

"What's going on?" Jessie looked first at Megan and then at Evan. "Why are you both so mad at each other? I thought you *liked* each other!"

"I guess not," said Megan sharply.

"Well," said Evan. But he couldn't think of a thing to say. It was as if every word in his brain had packed up and headed south to Florida for the winter.

"Show her the poem," said Jessie, reaching into her grocery bag.

Evan lunged for the bag and ripped it out of Jessie's hands so that she was left holding a single paper handle. "Hey! You can't do that!" she shouted, waving the torn handle, but Evan had already pulled out one of the newspapers and stuffed the grocery bag under his arm. He turned his back on the two girls and scanned the front page.

There it was.

Out in the open.

For everyone to see.

His poem. His love poem to Megan Moriarty.

Chapter 20
Copyright

copyright (n) the exclusive legal right of the author of a work to publish the work or allow someone else to publish it

Jessie took off after Evan. He was a much faster runner than she was, and he'd gotten a head start, so when she rounded the back of the school, he was out of sight. Jessie kept running until she came to the kindergarten playground, which was all the way on the other side of the school. The big kids weren't allowed on the kindergarten playground, but Jessie spotted Evan tucked into a corner of a wall, protected from the wind and out of sight of anyone in the school. He was reading one of her newspapers, with the grocery bag full of papers at his feet.

Jessie marched up to him and said, "Give me back my newspapers!"

"You're not handing these out," he said.

"Yes, I am!"

"No. You're. Not."

"You're not the boss of me, Evan Treski!" Jessie reached for the bag, but Evan grabbed it and pivoted, just like he did on the basketball court, and avoided her attack.

"Yeah, but I'm bigger and taller and OLDER. So too bad for you."

Jessie lunged at her brother. "They're mine, and I want them back!" Evan stiff-armed her and held the bag and the paper higher so that she couldn't get it.

"Quit it!" he said. "Let me *read!*"

Suddenly Jessie realized that Evan was her first reader. She stopped grabbing for the papers and instead watched him. This is what she had wanted all along: to write something that people couldn't put down.

Evan placed the bag of papers on the ground between his feet. He was a slow reader, and it took him a long time to get all the way to the end of the front-page article. Jessie watched as he flipped the paper over to the back page and read the answer to the mystery of the candy hearts. Then he looked at her, and the look on his face was one she knew well. He was about to explain something to her.

"Look, Jess," he said. "I should be really mad at you, and I am, but I know you just don't . . . get this. Here's the thing: You can't hand this paper out." He shuffled his feet together so that the grocery bag of newspapers was more safely wedged between his legs.

"Why?" she asked. She had the sinking feeling that she had done something that wasn't right. Something that other kids would have understood, but somehow she didn't. "Isn't it good?"

"Well, yeah, it's good," said Evan. "You did a great job writing up the mystery with all the clues." Evan nodded his head. "It's *really* good."

"So why can't I hand it out? I bet the other kids will want to read it, too."

"But you're going to *embarrass* Megan and probably get her in a lot of trouble. I mean, you tell everyone that she wrote on the bathroom door and that she handed out candy in school. She'll get sent to the principal for sure and maybe even suspended."

"Well, she should have thought about that before she did those things!" said Jessie. Jessie believed in following rules. Then again, here she was on the kindergarten playground. *And* she'd been planning to hand out her newspapers before Mrs. Overton had a chance to look at them. Which was not breaking a rule, really, but she knew she wasn't supposed to do it.

Jessie looked around quickly to see whether anyone had noticed that she was on the playground. Or whether Mrs. Overton was hunting for her.

"But do you really want to be the one who gets Megan in trouble? I mean, come on. It's Megan. She's the nicest person in the whole fourth grade."

It was true. Megan was always doing nice things for other people. She never excluded anyone or teased. She was the best friend Jessie had ever had besides Evan.

"And, Jess, in the survey results, you list names. You write in all the names of the kids that other kids have crushes on."

"But I don't tell who has a crush on who! I don't even know. The surveys were all anonymous."

"Yeah, but think how a kid might feel whose name isn't listed even once. Pretty lousy."

"Why?" asked Jessie. She really didn't get it. Why would anyone care if someone had a crush on them? It didn't make any sense to her. Then she thought about the missing survey and the name listed at the bottom of it: hers. She didn't know how she felt about *that,* but it was definitely a strange feeling.

"And, Jess!" Now Evan's voice did get angry— the same tone as when she'd gone into his room without his permission. "What about my poem? Huh? Where did you even *get* that?"

Jessie's voice came out very small. "From the trash."

"You took something out of my *trash can?*" Jessie could hear the heat in Evan's voice. She didn't want him to be angry. She had wanted to make him happy and proud.

"It looked like a turtle," she said. "And then I opened it up." She shook her head in confusion. "I thought you'd be happy to have your poem published. You should be proud that you write such good poetry. Mom said the poem you wrote for Grandma is one of the best poems she's ever read."

"But it's *private,* Jess," said Evan. "Don't you get it? I don't want anyone knowing that I write poetry. It's embarrassing."

Jessie didn't get it. Why would you want to hide a talent? Why wouldn't you want everyone to know how great you were? Jessie always wanted people to notice when she was the best.

"And besides," said Evan, "it's mine. *Mine.* Get it? And if I never want to show that poem to a single person my whole life, then that's what I'll do."

That was something Jessie could understand. You weren't allowed to print something if the author didn't want you to. It was called copyright, and it was the law.

"So what about . . . ?" Jessie pointed to the bag at Evan's feet. He stared back at her. "Can I hand out just a few?" Jessie's voice crumpled.

"Over my dead body," said Evan.

Jessie felt like the whole world was collapsing around her—the trees, the school building, the swing set, even Evan—shrinking and disappearing so that she was standing in emptiness. This is how it was for her when she just couldn't—*couldn't*—make sense of what was going on around her. The world became white and muffled and strange. That's when she liked to climb into her own bed and read one of her familiar books, where the story always turned out exactly the same way, so that Jessie knew what was coming next.

She looked at the paper in Evan's hands. Her beautiful paper. Everyone would want to read it. But she would have to kill it.

"You do it," she said. "I can't."

Evan put a hand on her shoulder. "Come on," he said. "We'll do it together."

Chapter 21
Jerks and Poets

juxtaposition (n) the placement of two very different words or ideas side by side to create a strong sense of contrast (but also connection) between the two

The hallway after recess was a tangle of kids and coats and boots and scarves as everyone hurried to put things away before going back into the classroom. Evan took his time, arranging and rearranging his things in his cubby. As usual, Megan was one of the last to come in.

When just a few students were left in the hall, Evan signaled Megan to wait by her cubby. Finally, they were alone.

Evan walked up to Megan, knowing that his face was getting redder by the second. He hoped she would think it was because it was so cold outside.

"I'm sorry," he said, "for acting like a jerk the last couple of days. The guys have all been giving me a hard time, and I just wanted them to leave me alone. I wasn't trying to be mean to you."

Megan nodded her head. "I've been getting teased a lot, too." She looked miserable. "I guess I've done some pretty dumb things lately. And I don't even know why I did them. Everything has felt so weird."

"I know what you mean." Evan's heart was beating a mile a minute. His right hand was hooked into his back pocket, and he could feel the folded-up paper he had tucked away there.

"It's just that . . ." Megan stopped and took a deep breath, then closed her eyes. "I like you, Evan."

Evan felt his heart leap in his chest and a sudden warm glow spread through his body and radiate out the tips of his fingers. For a moment, he wondered if he was floating above the ground. It was as if the happiness inside of him was a jet pack, lifting him gently into the air.

"But I *don't* want to go out with you!" Megan blurted out.

Whomp. The feeling of lightness vanished. Evan took half a step back, surprised. He opened his mouth. Nothing came out. There was a strange ringing in his ears, and he could feel his stomach starting to spin.

"It's no fun!" Megan stared at him, looking worried and upset. The spinning in his stomach kept going and going. The ringing in his ears was louder now, and he felt like his vision was being squeezed through a thin tube. He was looking down a long tunnel at her face, which was getting farther and farther away by the second. Everything was pulling away from him.

This was what he'd been waiting for. Dreading. This out-of-control feeling.

"Are you okay?" asked Megan.

Evan managed to nod his head.

"Are you mad?"

"No." The word came out so sad and lonely that Evan wished he could come up with a few more, just to keep it company.

"Then . . . can we be friends?"

Friends. Evan felt the spinning slow down a little.

"Sure. Friends," he croaked.

Megan smiled. "Good. That'll be way more fun." Her face rippled into smoothness, the way the surface of a pond settles back into itself after a stone is dropped.

Was it over? Evan wondered. He felt he should check his arms, his legs, his ribs, to see if he was still in one piece. Megan turned to go into the classroom.

"Wait!" he said. "I have something . . . there's this thing . . . I want to show you." He reached into his back pocket and pulled out *The 4-O Forum,* the only copy that hadn't been destroyed when he and Jessie had ripped up all the rest and thrown them in the Dumpster behind the school. "It's this thing . . . I wrote." He handed her the newspaper, folded so that his poem was in front.

Pony Girl
by Evan Treski

pony girl
flying by
always late
lately in my heart
you laugh your
happy laugh
you smile your
kindly smile
you gallop past
me standing still
dumb   struck

Megan read the poem silently. Evan concentrated on her ponytail. The ringing in his ears was quieter now, and his vision had gone back to normal.

Finally, Megan looked up at Evan. "Can I keep this?"

Evan nodded. "But only if you swear you'll never show it to anyone, your whole life."

"I swear," said Megan. She smiled.

Evan and Megan stood still. He wasn't sure what

to do next. They heard Mrs. Overton's voice floating out of the classroom—"Take out your science notebooks"—reminding them that it was time to get back to the business of school. Down the hall, Evan heard the bathroom door swing open, then bang shut. He didn't think much about it—until Scott Spencer flashed past them, and tore the newspaper out of Megan's hand.

"Sweet!" he shouted. "I've got the first copy!"

Chapter 22
"All the News That's Fit to Print"

"All the News That's Fit to Print" is the motto of the *New York Times* newspaper, printed on the front page of every issue; it means the paper won't print a story that is inaccurate, irresponsible, or harmful without a reason

"Quiet!" shouted Mrs. Overton.

Pandemonium had erupted in the classroom. Scott was waving the newspaper over his head, running circles around the bookcase that housed the gerbils, while Evan chased after him, shouting, "You'd better give it back, or else!"

Mrs. Overton clapped her hands once. "Scott, give me that paper, now!"

"He stole it from me!" yelled Megan.

"It's mine!" shouted Evan.

"Technically," said Jessie, "it's mine."

"Scott Spencer! This instant!"

Scott slowly walked over to Mrs. Overton, with the paper held open in front of him, greedily reading all the words he could before handing it to his teacher. Jessie could tell he wanted nothing more than to read the articles—*her* articles—and couldn't help feeling a little thrill to know that her paper was that good.

Jessie watched as Evan followed Scott and stood in front of their teacher. "Please, Mrs. Overton. Don't read it. It's private."

Mrs. Overton glanced up from the front page and looked straight at Jessie. "Jessie? What's going on here?"

Jessie raised both her hands and let them flop at

her side. "I wanted to write a blockbuster. I wanted to write something everyone would want to read." Jessie still didn't understand what was so wrong with that. But the kids in 4-O were like a pack of wolves closing in for the kill.

"Well, it looks like you've achieved your goal." Mrs. Overton's face did not look happy. Was she going to punish Jessie? Send her to the principal's office?

"Jessie *promised* she would tell us the results of the survey," said Tessa. "A promise is a promise."

"That's true," said Mrs. Overton. "And we all know what Langston says about promises." She pointed to the picture of Langston spitting out the words NEVER MAKE A PROMISE YOU CAN'T KEEP. ALWAYS KEEP THE PROMISES YOU MAKE.

"Mrs. Overton?" said Megan. "May I please read one of the letters from my advice column to the class?"

"Not right now, Megan."

"It's kind of important," she said.

"We don't want to hear your advice column!"

shouted Jack. "We want to find out who's in love!" The class started making all kinds of noise, but Mrs. Overton silenced them with one swoosh of her raised hand.

"Please?" said Megan. "It doesn't have anything to do with love."

Mrs. Overton allowed Megan to show her the letter she wanted to read and then gave her permission to read it out loud.

Dear Friend in 4-O,

I feel terrible. I did something I'm not supposed to do. Nobody knows. Every day I feel bad. I keep waiting to get caught. What should I do?

Signed,

Guilty in the Fourth Grade

Dear Guilty,

You're never going to feel better until you confess. Go to a grownup you trust and tell the truth. I guarantee you'll be happy you did.

Megan folded the paper and handed it back to her teacher. "I've decided to take my own advice. Mrs. Overton, I'm the one who handed out the candy hearts. I know I shouldn't have done it, but it was Valentine's Day, and I thought it wasn't such a bad thing to do."

Jessie looked around at her classmates. They were all frozen in their seats. It wasn't every day that someone admitted to being guilty of a crime.

"And also," continued Megan. She took a big breath. "I wrote something on one of the doors in the bathroom. I tried to clean it off, but I couldn't get it all. I'm *sorry!*" And then she exploded in tears. Great big, sloppy, wet tears. Jessie had never seen anyone cry like that before. It reminded her of a nature video she'd watched of a river dam breaking in a torrential rainstorm. Whoosh!

Mrs. Overton wrapped her arms around Megan and didn't seem to mind one bit that Megan was sopping the front of her shirt with tears and snot. For Jessie, that was proof that Mrs. Overton was a good teacher.

The rest of the class did their best not to watch. They looked at the floor or their own feet or their desks. Jessie looked up at the photo of Langston proclaiming, TO ERR IS HUMAN, TO FORGIVE, DIVINE.

When Megan quieted down, Mrs. Overton handed her a box of tissues and sent her to the nurse's office for a wet washcloth and to have a few quiet moments.

"Well," Mrs. Overton said. "Let's go sit on the rug." Everyone scrambled over to the rug, happy to leave behind the uncomfortable scene they'd just witnessed. Mrs. Overton settled into her rocking chair.

"First," said Mrs. Overton, "whose newspaper is this?"

Evan and Jessie both raised their hands.

"I wrote it," said Jessie, "but it's Evan's copy."

"We were *all* supposed to get copies, not just Evan," reminded Carly.

"Yeah, you promised, Jessie!" Most of the kids nodded their heads.

"Doesn't the paper belong to all of us, since we're

the ones who answered the survey questions?" asked David.

"I can't hand it out," said Jessie. "I put stuff in there that I shouldn't have."

"Stuff that isn't true?" asked Mrs. Overton.

"No, it's all true. Every word of it. It's just that there's a poem I put in that I didn't get permission to publish. So that's copyright infringement. And then there are names of people—and feelings might get hurt . . ." Jessie's voice trailed off. She was still unclear about the feelings part. The copyright law she understood, but the rest was a little muddy in her mind.

"So can't you tell us the results without using anyone's names? Just make it anonymous?" asked Salley.

"Yeah, and drop the poem," said Ryan. "Who cares about a poem?"

"I care about poems!" said Mrs. Overton. "But you can only publish a poem when you have the poet's permission. I guess you learned that the hard way, Jessie."

Jessie nodded. She felt sad and defeated. Her blockbuster had turned into a failure.

She looked at her teacher, sitting in her chair, the easel beside her. Mrs. Overton had begun reading the newspaper. She finished page one and turned to the back page. And kept on reading. It looked like she couldn't put it down.

"You did a wonderful job, Jessie," said Mrs. Overton, folding the newspaper in half. "You're not only a good investigative reporter and a forceful writer, you also know how to choose excellent poetry." She looked at Evan when she said this, and Jessie saw a smile dance across his face.

"Maybe . . ." said Jessie. "I could write a new edition? One that doesn't use anyone's name?"

Mrs. Overton rested her chin on her hand and rocked back and forth in her chair. They knew that this was her thinking pose, and the best thing to do was to keep quiet. She tapped her chin several times with her index finger, and then asked Jessie, "Will you include pie charts in the new edition?"

"Yes!" said Jessie. She just loved pie charts.

"And some poems?"

"A whole page," promised Jessie. "But only if the authors say it's okay."

"Then you may rewrite your paper, but you have to show it to me *before* you hand it out. Understood?"

"Absolutely!" said Jessie.

The 4-O Forum

Special Valentine's Day Issue

Survey Question #5:

What do you think is the best way to tell someone you have a crush on them?

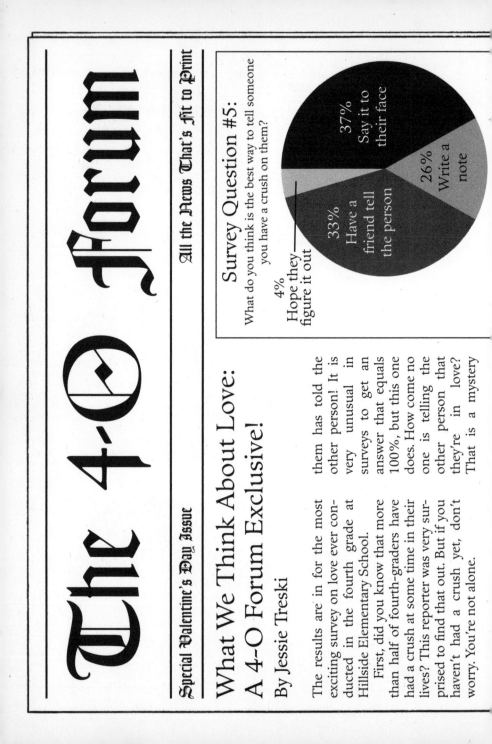

- 4% Hope they figure it out
- 33% Have a friend tell the person
- 26% Write a note
- 37% Say it to their face

What We Think About Love: A 4-O Forum Exclusive!

By Jessie Treski

The results are in for the most exciting survey on love ever conducted in the fourth grade at Hillside Elementary School.

First, did you know that more than half of fourth-graders have had a crush at some time in their lives? This reporter was very surprised to find that out. But if you haven't had a crush yet, don't worry. You're not alone.

them has told the other person! It is very unusual in surveys to get an answer that equals 100%, but this one does. How come no one is telling the other person that they're in love? That is a mystery

In 4-O, most of the kids have crushes now, and almost all those crushes are with someone in 4-O! So I guess if you fall in love, you're probably going to fall in love with someone in your own class.

Here is the most shocking statistic of all: Out of all the people who are in love in 4-O, not one of that can't be answered by this reporter.

How to tell your crush that you like them? Nobody seems to agree on this. The class is pretty evenly split: say it to their face, have a friend tell, write a note. One person in the class says that they just hope the person figures it out. (Note from this reporter:

That is a very bad way to communicate!)

So there you have it. Shocking, never-before-reported results on how the students of 4-O feel about love. Remember: You read it here first in *The 4-O Forum!*

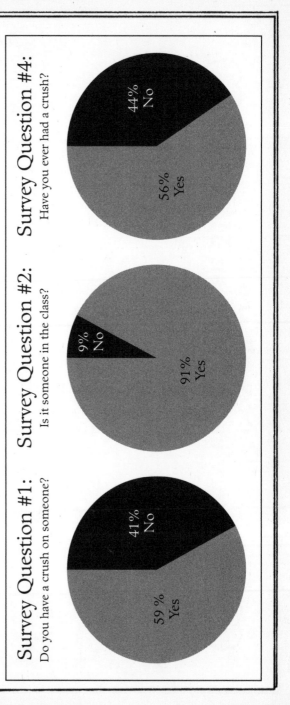

Survey Question #1:
Do you have a crush on someone?

59% Yes
41% No

Survey Question #2:
Is it someone in the class?

91% Yes
9% No

Survey Question #4:
Have you ever had a crush?

56% Yes
44% No

The Sweet Truth!
An Interview with Megan Moriarty

By Jessie Treski

On Monday, Valentine's Day, everyone in 4-O learned the truth about who has been giving out those candy hearts with mysterious messages written on them: Megan Moriarty! That means that Megan is officially the "sweetest" student in the whole fourth grade.

We caught up with Megan on the playground, and she agreed to answer some questions for *The 4-O Forum*. Here is the exclusive interview!

Q: What gave you the idea to give candy hearts to your classmates?

A: I always put candy in my valentines. Usually I put mini valentines. Usually I put mini candy hearts in our desks?

Q: How did you make the candy hearts?

A: That's easy. My uncle has a candy factory and he makes those personalized messages on candy hearts all the time. People give them out at weddings and birthday parties, so he's got this special printing machine that does it. You just type in the message and you can print out as many boxes as you want. The only tricky part is the message can't be more than two lines long and you can only have nine letters per line. So all the messages have to be really short.

Q: How did you get the candy hearts in our desks?

out any hearts on Tuesday or Wednesday. I didn't have a chance.

Q: Are you sorry you did it?

A: Honestly? Yes and no. I'm sorry I broke the rule. I know you're not supposed to break rules. But it's Valentine's Day! It only comes once a year. And candy is part of Valentine's Day. At least it is to me. And I think almost everyone really liked the hearts and the messages. I tried really hard to think about what was special about each person in the class. Everyone has a talent and I wanted to make them feel good about that. I wanted to say, "Hey, you're really great just the chocolate bars in because they're flat and they fit inside the envelope better. But when Mrs. Fletcher told us that we weren't allowed to hand out candy, I got kind of mad and I decided I was going to do it anyway. I know it was wrong to break the rule, but I don't think it's a very good rule.

A: That was the hardest part. I had to hand them out when the classroom was empty, so before school or after school or during recess. It was easy on the day Mrs. Feeney was there, but really hard with Mrs. Overton. She's sharp! Lucky for me, she's busy, too. But that's why I didn't hand

way you are!" So that's why I wrote special messages. Because Valentine's Day is about love, and part of love is liking yourself. I wanted everyone in 4-O to like themselves for a day.

They Came from Space! By Christopher Bay

A Friend in 4-O:
Advice for Fourth-Graders

By Megan Moriarty

Dear Friend in 4-O,

I feel terrible. I did something I'm not supposed to do. Nobody knows. Every day I feel bad. I keep waiting to get caught. What should I do?

Signed,
Guilty in the Fourth Grade

Dear Guilty,

You're never going to feel better until you confess. Go to a grownup you trust and tell the truth. I guarantee you'll be happy you did.

Dear Friend in 4-O,

Why do we have to make val-

time, but when I wear boots in the winter and run around on the playground, my feet really sweat. Then we come in from recess and take off our boots. Two kids told me my feet stink. Help me!

Signed,
Stinky and Sad

Dear Stinky,

First, those kids shouldn't tell you your feet smell bad. That's just rude. Second, I asked my mom about your problem, and she says there are things you can buy at the drugstore that take care of foot odor. Also, do you wash your feet every day? You should. So try those things out and hopefully your problem will

Sports Report

By Ryan Hart, Megan Moriarty, Jack Bagdasarian, and Tessa James

Here are the scores for the fourth grade girls' basketball games that were played this weekend:

Tigers 22 / Raptors 27
Polar Bears 5 / Wildcats 12
Eagles 31 / Hornets 19

Here are the scores for the fourth grade boys' basketball games that were played this weekend:

entines for everyone in the class? I don't like everyone. In fact, there are some kids I REALLY DON'T LIKE. Why should I make valentines for them?

Signed,
Tired of Making Valentines

Dear Tired,

I hear you! Making 27 valentines takes a lot of time. I spent about four hours making mine. But you *have* to give one to everyone so no one feels left out. How would *you* like it if you got just a few valentines? So here's my advice: Go to the store and buy a box of valentines. That way, you won't be so tired.

Dear Friend in 4–O,

This is really embarrassing, but my feet smell bad. Not all the

be solved.

Dear Friend in 4–O,

Because of all the poetry we've been reading in class, I've decided I want to be a poet when I grow up. Is that a real job? Do they make a lot of money? Is it hard to be a poet?

Signed,
In Love with Poetry

Dear In Love,

Your name says it all! If you love poetry, then you should be a poet. I asked Mrs. Overton, and she says poets don't make much money at all. But I say you should still do what you love. For instance, I love writing this advice column, and I don't get paid any money at all!

Bulls 19 / Hawks 22
Grizzlies 17 / Lakers 16
Pacers 39 / Celtics 20
Mavericks 7 / Thunder 27

All the indoor soccer games had to be canceled because the roof is still leaking at the indoor field. No one knows when it's going to be fixed.

Special Feature:
The Poetry Page

(All poems reprinted with the permission of the authors.)

Secrets
by Megan Moriarty

Some secrets are
Nice,
Like shiny, wet pearls
You string on a
Necklace.
One, two, three!

Some secrets feel like
Rocks
That hang from your
Heart.
They pull you down.

Some secrets are like
Needles.
They poke and poke and poke,
Wanting to be told.
Those are the most dangerous
Of all.

Stanley
by Malik Lewis

My dog is yellow and mellow.
He sits on my foot and crushes it!
I shout, "Get off my foot!"
But he's a dog, so
He just licks my face.
I love my dog.

Tepee in the Woods
by Evan Treski

You see
Broken branches
I see
A perfect palace

You see
Twisted string
I see
Someplace safe

You see
Nothing much
I see
A home

Poem for My Mom
by Jessie Treski
(with help from Evan Treski)

A vase is just a vase
Until you fill it with flowers.
A wand is just a stick
Without its magical powers.

A diamond's just a rock
Until you cut it right.
And a sunrise looks like nothing
Unless you start with night.

My mom is like a sunrise,
Warm and beautiful and gold.
My mom is like a diamond,
Strong and clear and bold.

But my mom is not a flower
That grows in rainy weather.
Instead, she's like the vase that
Holds us all together.

This Is Just to Say
by Jessie Treski

I have taken
the poem
you kept in
your room

and which
you were probably
trying
to keep private

Forgive me
it was so good
and I wanted
you to shine

(Note to the Reader: Mrs. Overton says it's okay for me to use William Carlos Williams's poem like this because everyone knows it's an imitation. A poem like this is called a parody, except a parody is supposed to be funny and my poem is serious.)

The Quarrel
by Eleanor Farjeon

I quarreled with my brother,
I don't know what about,
One thing led to another
And somehow we fell out.
The start of it was slight,
The end of it was strong,
He said he was right,
I knew he was wrong!

We hated one another.
The afternoon turned black.
Then suddenly my brother
Thumped me on the back,
And said, "Oh, come along!
We can't go on all night —
I was in the wrong."
So he was in the right.

(Note to the Reader: This poem is written by a famous, dead poet. It's my favorite poem of all time.)

Weather Data for the Month of January

Average high temperature	32°
Average low temperature	19°
Highest temperature	38°
Lowest temperature	4°
Total precipitation	3.36 inches
Relative humidity	64%

There were 9 clear days, 7 partly cloudy days, and 15 cloudy days.

Breaking News!

This just in!

Mrs. Overton has uncovered a startling fact:

E. E. Cummings's real name is . . .

Edward Estlin Cummings!

This reporter is not surprised that he kept that a secret!

POETRY TERMS

alliteration

When the same letter or sound occurs at the beginning of words
that are next to each other or nearby.
Examples:
heavenly hair
delicate and dainty daffodils
Be careful of cats' claws!

assonance

A poetic technique in which the middle sound of a word (usually
a vowel) is repeated in words that are next to the word or near it.
Examples:
get special letters
show old jokes
silly little kids

cliché

An overused expression that lacks power because it is so familiar.
Examples:
brave as a lion
the quiet before the storm
head over heels in love

consonance

The repetition of the same sounds (particularly consonants)
within words that are nearby.
Examples:
fancy ruffled cuffs
happily playing pandas
little Italian treats

hyperbole

An extremely exaggerated statement.
Examples:
She was so scared, she thought she would die.
I'm starving because I skipped breakfast.
I've got a ton of homework.

juxtaposition

The placement of two very different words or ideas side by side to create a strong sense of contrast (but also connection) between the two.
Examples:
My sweet, cuddly puppy has teeth that can tear a shoe to pieces.
He was the most selfish philanthropist I ever met.

metaphor

A figure of speech that says that one thing is another different thing as a way to compare the two and note their similarities.
Examples:
My little brother is a fly that keeps buzzing around my head.
The sunrise was a masterpiece of yellow and orange.

onomatopoeia

When a word sounds like the object it names or the sound that object makes.
Examples: *meow, knock knock, squirt*

personification

Giving lifelike characteristics to an inanimate object or an abstract idea; describing an object as if it were alive.
Examples:

The clock on the wall scolded me for being late with its angry tick-tock.
The flowers danced in the breeze.

simile

A comparison of one thing with another using "like" or "as."
Examples:
Her shouts were as loud as a trumpeting elephant.
The daffodils were yellow like melted butter.

slant rhyme

Two words that share the same final consonant sound or two
words that share the same middle vowel sound. They sound
almost like rhyming words, but not quite.
Examples:

> *"Hope" is the thing with feathers –*
> *That perches in the soul –*
> *And sings the tune without the words –*
> *And never stops – at all –*
>
> —Emily Dickinson

In this example "soul" and "all" create a slant rhyme.

★★★

POEMS

by E. E. Cummings

because it's

Spring
thingS

dare to do people

(& not
the other way

round)because it

's A
pril

Lives lead their own

persons(in
stead

of everybodyelse's)but

what's wholly
marvellous my

Darling

is that you &
i are more than you

& i(be

ca
us

e It's we)

MUSHROOMS
by Sylvia Plath

Overnight, very
Whitely, discreetly,
Very quietly

Our toes, our noses
Take hold on the loam,
Acquire the air.

Nobody sees us,
Stops us, betrays us;
The small grains make room.

Soft fists insist on
Heaving the needles,
The leafy bedding,

Even the paving.
Our hammers, our rams,
Earless and eyeless,

Perfectly voiceless,
Widen the crannies,
Shoulder through holes. We

Diet on water,
On crumbs of shadow,
Bland-mannered, asking

Little or nothing.
So many of us!
So many of us!

We are shelves, we are
Tables, we are meek,
We are edible,

Nudgers and shovers
In spite of ourselves.
Our kind multiplies:

We shall by morning
Inherit the earth.
Our foot's in the door.

TOAD
by Valerie Worth

When the flowers
Turned clever, and
Earned wide
Tender red petals
For themselves,

When the birds
Learned about feathers,
Spread green tails,
Grew cockades
On their heads,

The toad said:
Someone has got
To remember
The mud, and
I'm not proud.

BUG
by Malik

I dug a bug from under the rug.
The bug said hi and looked me in the eye.
I hugged my bug.
Bad idea!
Bye-bye bug.

FOG
by Carl Sandburg

The fog comes
on little cat feet.

It sits looking
over harbor and city
on silent haunches
and then moves on.

COUNTING RIBS
by Mrs. Overton

your head
too weak to lift I
lay my own alongside
yours and run my hand
across the silky familiar side of you
fingers feeling bone beneath
one   two   three

                                   breathe
four   five   six

                                   please
seven   eight   nine

                                   breathe

counting to keep my
eyes from crying my
heart from breaking
out
of its own ribbed cage

breathe   please   breathe

GRANDMA
by Evan Treski

a tree(doesn't have)
knees that creak
> but
> Grandma
> does

a tree(wouldn't forget)
my name
> but
> Grandma
> did

a tree(stands tall)
and proud
and good
> and
> Grandma
> is

> a tree

by E. E. Cummings

i carry your heart with me(i carry it in
my heart)i am never without it(anywhere
i go you go,my dear;and whatever is done
by only me is your doing,my darling)
                                i fear
no fate(for you are my fate,my sweet)i want
no world(for beautiful you are my world,my true)
and it's you are whatever a moon has always meant
and whatever a sun will always sing is you

here is the deepest secret nobody knows
(here is the root of the root and the bud of the bud
and the sky of the sky of a tree called life;which grows
higher than soul can hope or mind can hide)
and this is the wonder that's keeping the stars apart

i carry your heart(i carry it in my heart)

PONY GIRL
by Evan Treski

pony girl
flying by
always late
lately in my heart
you laugh your
happy laugh
you smile your
kindly smile
you gallop past
me standing still
dumb   struck

THE QUARREL
by Eleanor Farjeon

I quarreled with my brother,
I don't know what about,
One thing led to another
And somehow we fell out.
The start of it was slight,
The end of it was strong,
He said he was right,
I knew he was wrong!

We hated one another.
The afternoon turned black.
Then suddenly my brother
Thumped me on the back,
And said, "Oh, come along!
We can't go on all night —
I was in the wrong."
So he was in the right.

ACKNOWLEDGMENTS

Always, always, and ever again, thanks to my writers' group: Carol Peacock, Sarah Lamstein, Tracey Fern, and Mary Atkinson. A very special thanks to the teachers and students who have taken part in, contributed to, shaped, and brought life to the poetry residency I teach in elementary schools across the country, in particular my friends at Pine Hill Elementary School, who have been getting all jazzed up about poetry with me for almost a decade. I also want to thank Amy Cicala, fourth grade teacher at Hillside Elementary School, for sitting down with me and having a frank and enlightening discussion about love (and other matters) in the fourth grade, and Michael Kascak, principal at Hillside, who shared with me his school (and life) philosophy: "Be kind and do your work." Thanks again to Ryle Sammut, who contributed Evan's handwriting to the artwork in the book, and to Marisa Ih, who came up with the clever title "The Sweet Truth." A mother's thank-you goes to Mae Davies, who wrote me a poem when she was Evan's age that began, "A vase is just a vase / 'Til you put flowers in it." To the "Permissions Mavens" at Houghton Mifflin Harcourt who shepherded me through the process of securing permissions for this book—Katie Huha and Mary Dalton-Hoffman—I can only say that I owe you my sanity and I am forever in awe of your abilities. I also bow down before the talented team at HMH who make books appear out of air: the gifted Cara Llewellyn, rock-steady Christine Krones, and nimble Ann-Marie Pucillo. And if at this point in the unwieldy Acknowledgments paragraph I were able to blow a trumpet, shine a spotlight, drop balloons, and strike up a loud brass band, I would do all that to say thank you, thank you, thank you to my editor Ann Rider. *i carry your heart(i carry it in my heart)*.

PERMISSIONS CREDITS

"Because it's". Copyright © 1963, 1991 by The Trustees for the E.E. Cummings Trust, "i carry your heart with me(i carry it in." Copyright 1952, © 1980, 1991 by the Trustees for the E.E. Cummings Trust, from COMPLETE POEMS: 1904-1962 by E.E. Cummings, edited by George J. Firmage. Used by permission of Liveright Publishing Corporation.

"The Quarrel" from SILVER SAND AND SNOW by Eleanor Farjeon. Reprinted by permission of David Higham Associates, London.

"Mushrooms" from THE COLOSSUS AND OTHER POEMS by Sylvia Plath, copyright © 1957, 1958, 1959, 1960, 1961, 1962 by Sylvia Plath. Used by permission of Alfred A. Knopf, a division of Random House, Inc. Any third party use of this material, outside of this publication, is prohibited. Interested parties must apply directly to Random House, Inc. for permission.

"Fog" from CHICAGO POEMS by Carl Sandburg, copyright 1916 by Holt, Rinehart and Winston and renewed 1944 by Carl Sandburg, reproduced by permission of Houghton Mifflin Harcourt Publishing Company.

The poem "TOAD" from ALL THE SMALL POEMS AND FOURTEEN MORE © 1994 by Valerie Worth. Reprinted by permission of Farrar, Straus, and Giroux, LLC. All Rights Reserved.